The Dawn of the World

Myths and Weird Tales Told by the Mewan [Miwok] Indians of California

By

Clinton Hart Merriam

First published in 1910

Published by Left of Brain Books

Copyright © 2023 Left of Brain Books

ISBN 978-1-396-32668-4

First Edition

PUBLISHER'S PREFACE

About the Book

The Dawn of the World Myths and Weird Tales Told by the Mewan [Miwok] Indians of California, by C. Hart Merriam [1910].

About the Author

Clinton Hart Merriam (1855 - 1942)

"Clinton Hart Merriam (December 5, 1855-March 19, 1942) was an American zoologist, ornithologist, entomologist and ethnographer.

He was born in New York City in 1855. His father, Clinton Levi Merriam, was a U.S. congressman. He studied biology and anatomy at Yale University and went on to obtain an M.D. from the School of Physicians and Surgeons at Columbia University in 1879.

In 1886, he became the first chief of the Division of Economic Ornithology and Mammalogy of the United States Department of Agriculture, predecessor to the National Wildlife Research Center and the United States Fish and Wildlife Service. He was one of the original founders of the National Geographic Society in 1888. He developed the "life zones" concept to classify biomes found in North America.

In 1899, he helped railroad magnate E. H. Harriman to organize an exploratory voyage along the Alaska coastline.

Some species of animals that bear his name are Merriam's Wild Turkey Meliagris gallopavo meriami, the now extinct Merriam's Elk Cervus elaphus merriami, and Merriam's Chipmunk Tamias merriami. Much of his detail-oriented taxonomy continues to be influential within mammalogical and ornithological circles.

Later in life, funded by the Harriman family, Merriam's focus shifted to studying and assisting the Native American tribes in the western United

States. His contributions on the myths of central California and on ethnogeography were particularly noteworthy."

(Quote from wikipedia.org)

CONTENTS

PREFACE

IT is our custom to go abroad for the early beliefs of mankind and to teach our children the mythologies of foreign lands, unmindful of the wealth and beauty of our American folk-tales. The present collection invites attention to the unique and entertaining character of the myths of some of our California Indians.

These tales were told me by the Indians of a single stock, the Mewan, the tribes of which are confined to central California and have no known relatives in any part of the world. They have been little visited by ethnologists and during the few years that have passed since the tales were collected, several of the tribes have become extinct.

The myths are related by the old people after the first rains of the winter season, usually in the ceremonial roundhouse and always at night by the dim light of a small flickering fire. They constitute the religious history of the tribe, and from time immemorial have been handed down by word of mouth; from generation to generation they have been repeated, without loss and without addition.

The conceptions of the Indians concerning the forces of nature and the character and attributes of the early inhabitants of the earth differ so radically from our own that an explanation seems necessary. This is supplied by the Introduction, which is intended to give the reader the view point necessary for the full appreciation and enjoyment of the tales.

C. HART MERRIAM

Washington, D.C., January, 1910.

INTRODUCTION

THE mythology of the Indians of California goes back much farther than our mythology: it goes back to the time of the FIRST PEOPLE--curious beings who inhabited the country for a long period before man was created.

The myths of the Mewan tribes abound in magic, and many of them suggest a moral. They tell of the doings of the FIRST PEOPLE--of their search for fire; of their hunting exploits; of their adventures, including battles with giants and miraculous escapes from death; of their personal attributes, including selfishness and jealousy and their consequences; of the creation of Indian people by a divinity called Coyote-man; and finally of the transformation of the FIRST PEOPLE into animals and other objects of nature.

Some explain the origin of thunder, lightning, the rainbow, and other natural phenomena; some tell of a flood, when only the tops of the highest mountains broke the waves; others of a cheerless period of cold and darkness before the acquisition of the coveted heat and light-giving substance, which finally was stolen and brought home to the people.

FUNDAMENTAL ELEMENTS OF MEWAN MYTHOLOGY

The more important features of Mewan Mythology may be summarized as follows:

The existence of a FIRST PEOPLE, beings who differed materially from the present Indians, and who, immediately before the present Indians were created, were transformed into animals, trees, rocks, and in some cases into stars and other celestial bodies or forces--for even Sah'-win-ne the Hail, and Nuk'-kah the Rain were FIRST PEOPLE.

The preëxistence of Coyote-man, the Creator, a divinity of unknown origin and fabulous 'magic,' whose influence was always for good. [1]

The existence (in some cases preëxistence) of other divinities, notably Wek'-wek the Falcon, grandson and companion of Coyote-man, Mol'-luk the Condor, father of Wek'-wek, and Pe-tā'-le the Lizard, who, according to several tribes, assisted Coyote-man in the creation of Indian people.

The possession of supernatural powers or magic by Coyote-man, Wek'-wek, and others of the early divinities, enabling them to perform miracles.

The prevalence of universal darkness, which in the beginning overspread the world and continued for a very long period.

The existence at a great distance of a primordial heat and light giving substance indifferently called fire, sun, or morning--for in the early myths these were considered identical or at least interconvertible. [2]

The presence of a keeper or guardian of the fire, it being foreseen by its first possessors that because of its priceless value efforts would be made to steal it.

The theft of fire, which in all cases was stolen from people or divinities living at a great distance.

The preservation of the stolen fire by implanting it in the oo'-noo or buckeye tree, where it was and still is, accessible to all.

The power of certain personages or divinities--as Ke'-lok the North Giant, Sah'-te the Weasel-man, and O-wah'-to the Big-headed Lizard--to use fire as a weapon by sending it to pursue and overwhelm their enemies.

---

[1] Partial exceptions, doubtless a result of contact with neighboring stocks, occur in two tribes: the Wi'-pa say that Coyote-man boasted beyond his powers; and the Northern Mewuk say that he was selfish.

[2] A partial exception is the belief of the Hoo-koo-e-ko of Tomales Bay who say that in the beginning the source of light was He'-koo-las the Sun-woman, whose body was covered with shining abalone shells.

The conception of the sky as a dome-shaped canopy resting on the earth and perforated, on the sides corresponding to the cardinal points, with four holes which are continually opening and closing. A fifth hole, in the center of the sky, directly overhead, is spoken of by some tribes.

The existence, at or near the north hole in the sky, of Thunder Mountain, a place of excessive cold.

The presence of people on top of or beyond the sky.

The presence of people on the underside of the earth. (This belief may not be held by all the tribes.)

The existence of Rock Giants, who dwelt in caves and carried off and devoured people.

The tendency of the dead to rise and return to life on the third or fourth day after death.

The prevention of the rising of the dead and their return to life by Meadowlark-man, who would not permit immortality.

The creation of real people, the ancestors of the present Indians, by the transformation of feathers, sticks, or clay. [1] Of these beliefs, origin from feathers is the most distinctive and widespread, reaching from Fresno Creek north to Clear Lake. [2]

The completion and perfection of newly created man by the gift of five fingers from Pe-tā'-le the Lizard-man, who, having five himself, understood their value.

---

[1] A single exception has been found: The Northern Mewuk account for people by the gradual evolution of the offspring of the Cougar-man and his wives, the Grizzly Bear-woman and the Raccoon-woman.

[2] The widespread belief in the origin of people from feathers accounts for the reverence shown feathers by some of the tribes. This feeling sometimes manifests itself in a great fear or dread lest the failure to show proper respect for feathers, or to observe punctiliously certain prescribed acts in connection with the use of feather articles on ceremonious occasions, be followed by illness or disaster. This awe of feathers, I have observed among the Hoo'-koo-e'-ko of Tomales Bay, the Tu'-le-yo'-me of Lake County, and the Northern Mewuk of Calaveras County.

MINOR BELIEFS

In addition to the more fundamental elements of Mewan Mythology there are numerous beliefs which, while equally widespread, vary with the tribe and are of less importance. Among these are the tales of the elderberry tree--the source of music and other beneficent gifts to the people. In the beginning of the world the elderberry tree, as it swayed to and fro in the breeze, made sweet music for the Star-maidens and kept them from falling asleep; its wood served Tol'-le-loo for a flute when he put the Valley People to sleep so that he might steal the fire; and today it serves for flutes and clapper-sticks in nearly all the tribes and plays a vital part in their ceremonial observances.

Other widespread beliefs are that the great hunters of the FIRST PEOPLE were the Raven, Cougar, and Gray Fox; that Mermaids or Water-women, who sometimes harm people, dwell in the ocean and in certain rivers; that the echo is the Lizard-man talking back; that certain divinities have the magic power of accomplishing their desires by wishing; and that the red parts of birds--as the chin of the Humming-bird, the underside of the wings and tail of the western Flicker, the breast of the Robin, and the red head of the Mountain Tanager and certain others, indicate that these parts have been in contact with the fire.

LOCAL OR TRIBAL MYTHS

There are also numerous local beliefs, confined to particular tribes or groups of tribes. Thus the Inneko tribes, those living north of San Francisco Bay, tell of a flood; the two coast tribes say that in the beginning the Divinity Coyote-man came to America from the west by crossing the Pacific Ocean on a raft; the Northern Mewuk believe that they came from the Cougar-man and Grizzly Bear woman; the Tu'-le-yo'-me say that when Sah'-te set the world on fire, Coyote-man made the flood and put out the fire. Other local myths are that Wek'-wek was born of a rock; that Chā'-ke the Tule-wren, a poor despised orphan boy, shot out the sun, leaving the world in total darkness; that His'-sik the Skunk, whose greed and oppression were intolerable, was destroyed by the superior cunning of Too'-wik the Badger; that He'-koo-lās the Sun-woman owed her brilliancy to a coat of resplendent abalone shells; that the We'-ke-wil'-lah brothers, tiny Shrews, stole the fire from Kah'-kah-te the Crow and by touching a bug to the spark made the first firefly. Numerous others will be found in the tales--in fact every tribe has myths of its own. Furthermore, in the general mythologies, each band or subtribe has slight variants, so that even the creation myths, as related by different bands, present minor differences.

The repeated mention in the mythologies of certain objects and practices (as the ceremonial roundhouse, the use of the stone mortar and pestle for grinding acorns, the use of baskets for cooking, the use of the bow and arrow and sling in hunting, the practice of gambling by means of the hand-game, and many others) proves that these objects and observances are not of recent introduction but were among the early possessions and practices of the Mewan tribes.

It is important to discriminate between the real mythology of a people, the tales that deal with personages and events of the very remote past, and present day myths, which deal with happenings of the hour or of the very recent past. Some of the present day myths of the Mewan tribes may be found in a separate chapter at the end of the volume.

CHARACTERISTICS OF THE FIRST PEOPLE PERPETUATED IN THEIR FINAL FORMS

The names of individual personages among the FIRST PEOPLE were carried on to the animals, objects, or forces which these people became at the time of their final transformation, and are still borne by them. Hence in the accompanying stories the names of the various animals and objects should not be understood as referring to them as they exist today but to their remote ancestors among the FIRST PEOPLE. Whatever their original form-- and the Indian conception seems to picture them as half human--the distinctive attributes of the FIRST PEOPLE were in the main handed down to the animals and objects they finally became.

Thus Oo-soom'-ma-te's fondness for acorns was not diminished by her transformation into the Grizzly Bear; Yu'-wel's skill as a hunter did not forsake him when he turned into the Gray Fox; He-le'-jah's prowess as a deer slayer lost nothing when he changed to the Cougar; and Too'-pe's nocturnal ways were not abandoned when she became the Kangaroo Rat. Similarly, Ko-to'-lah's habit of jumping into the water is perpetuated by the Frog; Too'-wek's preëminence as a digger is still conspicuous in the Badger; To-to'-ka-no's loud penetrating voice is even now a signal characteristic of the Sandhill Crane; while the swiftness of flight of Wek'-wek, Hoo-loo'-e, and Le'-che-che who could shoot through the holes in the sky, ever opening and closing with lightning rapidity, are today marked attributes of the Falcon, Dove, and Humming-bird. So it is also with Nuk'-kah the Shower and Sah'-win-ne the Hail, who were sent to overtake and capture a fleeing enemy and who to this day are noted for the velocity and force of their movements. Such cases might be multiplied almost indefinitely.

DISTRIBUTION OF THE MEWAN INDIANS [1]

The territory of the Mewan tribes comprised the lower slopes and foothills of the Sierra Nevada between the Cosumnes River on the north and Fresno Creek on the south, with the adjacent plain from the foothills to Suisun Bay, and also two smaller disconnected areas north of San Francisco Bay-- one in the interior, reaching from Pope Valley to the south end of Clear Lake, the other on the coast, from Golden Gate northerly nearly to the mouth of Russian River. (See accompanying map.)

At present the vanishing remnants of the Mewuk tribes are scattered over their old territory on the west flank of the Sierra; the handful that remain of the Tuleyome tribe are gathered in a small rancheria on Putah Creek in Lake County; while the sole survivors of the Hookooeko and Olamentko tribes (in each case a single person) still cling to their original homes on Tomales and Bodega Bays.

DIFFERENCES IN LANGUAGE

The California tribes are stationary, not nomadic; they have lived for thousands of years in the places they now occupy, or did occupy until driven away by the whites; and during this long period of isolation they have evolved different languages for even among tribes of the same linguistic group the differences in language are often so great that members of one tribe cannot understand the speech of another. [2]

---

[1] For a detailed account of the distribution of these tribes see my article entitled, "Distribution and Classification of the Mewan stock of California," American Anthropologist, vol. ix, 338-357.

[2] Hence in the accompanying myths the name of the same personage or animal differs according to the tribe speaking. Thus Coyote-man may be Ah-hā'-le, Os-sā'-le, O-lā'-choo, O-lā'-nah, O-let'-te, Ol'-le, or O'-ye. Similarly, the Humming-bird may be Koo-loo'-loo, Koo-loo'-pe, or Le'-che-che. The Falcon or Duck-hawk, on the

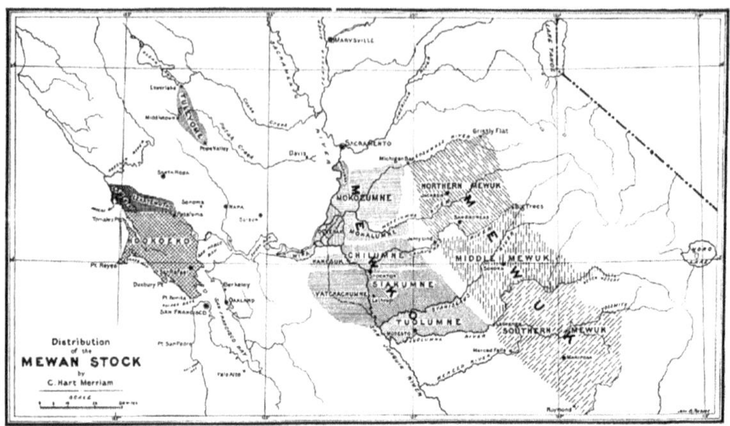

Distribution of the Mewan Stock

As the languages of the tribes composing the Mewan stock show varying degrees of kinship, so their myths exhibit varying relationships. Those of the Sierra region are the most closely interrelated; those of the San Francisco Bay region and northward the most divergent.

other hand, is Wek'-wek in all the tribes. This is because his name is derived from his cry. Many other Indian names of mammals and birds have a similar origin.

NOTE

THE accompanying illustrations are from paintings made expressly for the present collection of Myths by Edwin W. Deming of New York and Charles J. Hittell of San Francisco.

Of the stories here published, only a few are complete, and several consist of the merest fragments. All however are of ethnologic value, for even those expressing a single idea may prove of service in tracing relationship. In preparing them for the press my aim has been to reproduce them in simple English, adhering as closely as possible to the form in which they were told me by the Indians. Certain brief passages and repetitions have been omitted; nothing has been added.

All the Indian words, whether tribal names or names of objects, are written in simple phonetic English. The letter a, when unmarked, has the sound of a in fat; a long (ā) has the sound of a in fate; and the ah sound is always spelled, ah.

PART I: ANCIENT MYTHS

STORIES OF THE FIRST PEOPLE--PEOPLE WHO LIVED BEFORE REAL PEOPLE WERE CREATED

THE Mewuk tribes, those inhabiting the western slopes and foothills of the Sierra, call the ancient myths oo'-ten-ne or oot'-ne, meaning the history of the FIRST PEOPLE. (The Northern Mewuk say oo'-ten nas'-se-sa.) In this connection it may be significant that the name of Bower Cave, the home of Too'-le and He-le'-jah, two great chiefs of the FIRST PEOPLE, is Oo'-tin.

HOW WIT'-TAB-BAH THE ROBIN GOT HIS RED BREAST

A LONG time ago the world was dark and cold and the people had no fire. Wit'-tab-bah the Robin learned where the fire was and went on a far journey to get it. After he had traveled a great distance he came to the place and stole it and carried it back to the people. Every night on the way he lay with his breast over it to keep it from getting cold; this turned his breast red. Finally he reached home with it and gave it to the people. Then he made the Sun out of it, but before doing this he put some into the oo'-noo tree (the buckeye) so the people could get it when they needed it. From that day to this all the people have known that when they want fire they can get it by rubbing an oo'-noo stick against a piece of dry wood; this makes the flame come out.

HOW AH-HA'-LE STOLE THE SUN FOR THE VALLEY PEOPLE

As told by the Mariposa Mewuk

TO'-TO'-KAN-NO the Sandhill Crane was chief of the Valley People and Ah-hā'-le, the Coyote-man lived with him. Their country was cold and dark and full of fog.

Ah-hā'-le was discontented and traveled all about, trying to find a better place for the people. After a while he came to the Foothills Country where it began to be light. He went on a little farther and for the first time in his life saw trees, and found the country dry and warm, and good to look at. Soon he saw the Foothills People and found their village. He was himself a magician or witch doctor, so he turned into one of the Foothills People and mingled with them to see what they had and what they were doing. He saw that they had fire, which made light and became Wut'-too the Sun. He saw also that there were both men and women, that the women pounded acorns and cooked acorn mush in baskets, and that everybody ate food. He ate with them and learned that food was good.

When his belly was full he went home and told the chief To-to'-kan-no that he had found a good place where there were people who had the sun and moon and stars, and women, and things to eat. He then asked To-to'-kan-no, "What are we going to do? Are we going to stay down here in the dark and never eat? The people up there have wives and children; the women make acorn soup and other things; the men have light and can see to hunt and kill deer. We live down here in the dark and have no women and nothing to eat. What are we going to do?"

Chief To-to'-kan-no answered; "Those things are not worth having. I don't want the Sun, nor the light, nor any of those things. Go back up there if you want to."

Ah-hā'-le went back to the foothills and did as he had done before, and liked the country and the people. Then he returned and told To-to'-kan-no what he had told him before, and again asked, "What are we going to do? Can't we buy the Sun? The people up there send the Sun away nights so they can sleep, and it comes back every day so they can see to hunt and get things to eat and have a good time. I like the Sun. Let us buy him."

To-to'-kan-no answered, "What is the matter with you? What would you do with the Sun; how would you use it?" But Ah-hā'-le was not satisfied. He went back to the Foothills People several times, and the more he saw of the Sun the more he wanted it. But To-to'-kan-no always said he did not want it. Finally however he told Ah-hā'-le that he might go and find out what it would cost.

The Foothills Country. "Ah-ha'-le went on a little farther and for the first time in his life saw trees, and found the country dry and good to look at."

Ah-hā'-le went and found that the people would not sell it; that if he got it he would have to steal it. And this would be very difficult, for Ah-wahn'-dah the Turtle, keeper of the Sun, was most watchful; he slept only a few minutes at a time and then stood up and looked around; besides, when he slept he always kept one eye open. If Ah-hā'-le moved his foot Ah-wahn'-dah would pick up his bow and arrow. Ah-hā'-le felt discouraged and did not know what to do. He feared that in order to get the Sun he would have to take Ah-wahn'-dah also.

But he decided to try once more, so he went again and turned into a man of the Foothills People. About four o'clock in the afternoon all the hunters went off to hunt deer. Then Ah-hā'-le turned into a big oak limb and fell down on the trail, and wished that Ah-wahn'-dah the Sun's keeper would come along first. And so it happened, for soon Ah-wahn'-dah came along the trail, saw the crooked limb, picked it up, carried it home on his shoulder, and threw it down on the ground. After supper he picked it up again and threw it against the fire, but it would not lay flat for it was very crooked and always turned up. Finally Ah-wahn'-dah threw it right into the middle of the fire. Then he looked all around, but could not see anybody. Ah-hā'-le who was now in the fire did not burn, but kept perfectly still and wished the keeper, Ah-wahn'-dah, would go to sleep.

Soon this happened and Ah-wahn'-dah fell fast asleep. Then Ah-hā'-le changed back into his own form and seized the Sun and ran quickly away with it.

Ah-wahn'-dah awoke and saw that the Sun was gone and called everybody to come quick and find it, but they could not for Ah-hā'-le had taken it down through the fog to the Valley People.

But when the Valley People saw it they were afraid and turned away from it, for it was too bright and hurt their eyes, and they said they could never sleep.

Ah-hā'-le took it to the chief, To-to'-kan-no, but To-to'-kan-no would not have it; he said he didn't understand it; that Ah-hā'-le must make it go, for he had seen how the Foothills People did it.

When To-to'-kan-no refused to have anything to do with the Sun, Ah-hā'-le was disappointed, for he had worked very hard to get it.

Still he said, "Well, I'll make it go."

So he carried the Sun west to the place where the sky comes down to the earth, and found the west hole in the sky, and told Wut'-too to go through the hole and down under the earth and come up on the east side and climb up through the east bole in the sky, and work in two places--to make light over the Foothills People first, then come on down and make light over the

Valley People, and then go through the west hole again and back under the earth so the people could sleep, and to keep on doing this, traveling all the time.

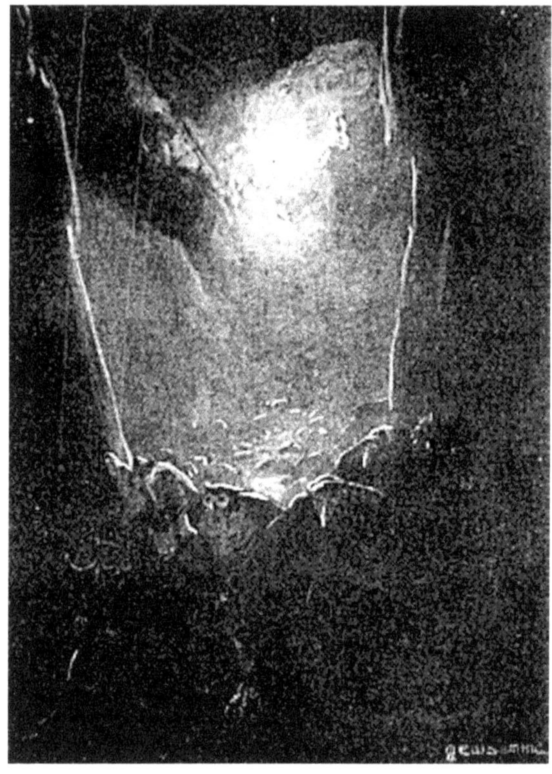

The Valley People shrinking from the Light. "Ah-ha-le stole the Sun and brought it down through the fog and darkness to the Valley People, but they were afraid and turned from it."

Wut'-too the Sun did as he was told. Then To-to'-kan-no and all the Valley People were glad, because they could see to hunt, and the Foothills People were satisfied too, for they had the light in the daytime so they could see, and at night the Sun went away so all the people could sleep.

After this, when the Sun was in the sky as it is now, all the FIRST PEOPLE turned into animals.

HOW AH-HA'-LE STOLE THE MORNING

As told by the Chowchilla Mewuk

IN the long ago time the world was dark and there was no fire. The only light was the Morning, [1] and it was so far away in the high mountains of the east that the people could not see it; they lived in total darkness. The chief We'-wis-sool, the Golden Eagle, felt very badly because it was always dark and cried all the time.

Ah-hā'-le the Coyote-man made up his mind to go and get the Morning in order that the people might have light. So he set out on the long journey to the east, up over the high mountains, saying, "I'm going to get the Morning."

Finally he came to Ah-wahn'-dah the Turtle. Ah-wahn'-dah was guardian of the Morning; he wore a big basket on his back. When Ah-hā'-le came close to Ah-wahn'-dah he was afraid something would catch him and carry him off. He said to himself, "I'm going to turn myself into a log of wood so I'll be too heavy to be carried off," and he turned into a big dry limb. Ah-wahn'-dah the Turtle put fire to the limb, but it would not burn; then he fell asleep. When the Guardian had gone to sleep Ah-hā'-le got up and said, "Now I'm going to get the Morning." So he changed back into his own form and put out his foot and touched the Morning, and it growled. He then caught hold of it and jumped quickly and ran away with it and brought it back to his people.

When he arrived he said to We'-wis-sool the Eagle, "How are you?"

We'-wis-sool answered, "All right," but was still crying because it was dark.

Then Ah-hā'-le said, "Tomorrow morning it is going to be light," but We'-wis-sool did not believe him.

---

[1] Morning, in this story, is obviously synonymous with sun and light, and probably with fire also, as in the preceding story.

In the morning Ah-hā'-le gave the people the light. We'-wis-sool was very happy and asked Ah-hā'-le where he got it, and Ah-hā'-le told him. Then the people began to walk around and find things to eat, for now they could see.

HOW TOL'-LE-LOO GOT THE FIRE FOR THE MOUN-TAIN PEOPLE

WEK'-WEK the Falcon and We'-pi-ah'-gah the Golden Eagle were Chiefs of the Valley People. Among the members of their tribe were Mol'-luk the Condor; Hoo'-a-zoo the Turkey Buzzard; Hoo-loo'-e the Dove; Te-wi'-yu the Red-shafted Flicker, who must have been very close to the fire--as any one can see from the red under his wings and tail, and Wit'-tab-bah the red-breasted Robin, who was keeper of the fire. There were also Hah-ki'-ah the Elk, Hal'-loo-zoo the Antelope, Sahk'-mum-chah the Cinnamon Bear, and others.

The Mountain People were in darkness and wanted fire but did not know where it was or how to get it. O-lā-choo the Coyote-man tried hard to find it but did not succeed. After a while Tol'-le-loo the White-footed Mouse discovered the fire and the Mountain People sent him to steal it.

Tol'-le-loo took his flute (loo'-lah) of elderberry wood and went down into the Valley and found the big roundhouse of Wek'-wek and We-pi-ah'-gah and began to play. The people liked the music and asked him to come inside. So he went in and played for them. Soon all the people felt sleepy. Wit'-tab-bah the Robin was sure that Tol'-le-loo had come to steal the fire, so he spread himself over it and covered it all up in order to hide it, and it turned his breast red. But Tol'-le-loo kept on playing his flute--and in a little while all the people were sound asleep; even Wit'-tab-bah could not keep awake.

Then Tol'-le-loo ran up to Wit'-tab-bah and cut a little hole in his wing and crawled through and stole the fire and put it inside his flute. When he had done this he ran out with it and climbed up to the top of the high mountain called Oo'-yum-bel'-le (Mount Diablo) and made a great fire which lighted up all the country till even the blue mountains far away in the east [the Sierra Nevada range] could be seen. Before this all the world was dark.

When Wek'-wek awoke he saw the fire on Oo'-yum-bel'-le and knew that Tol'-le-loo had stolen it. So he ran out and followed him and after a while caught him.

Tol'-le-loo said, "Look and see if I have the fire."

Wek'-wek looked but could not find it, for it was inside the flute. Then Wek'-wek pitched Tot'-le-loo into the water and let him go.

Tol'-le-loo got out and went east into the mountains and carried the fire in his flute to the Mountain People; then he took it out of the flute and put it on the ground and covered it with leaves and pine needles and tied it up in a small bundle.

Tol'-le-loo the Mouse playing his flute and putting the Valley People to sleep so he can steal the Fire

O-lā'-choo the Coyote smelled it and wanted to steal it. He came up and pushed it with his nose and was going to swallow it when it suddenly shot up into the sky and became the Sun.

O-lā'-choo sent Le'-che-che the Humming-bird, and another bird, named Le-che-koo'-tah-mah, who also had a long bill, after it, but they could not catch it and came back without it.

The people took the fire that was left and put it into two trees, oo'-noo the buckeye and mon'-o-go the incense cedar, where it still is and where it can be had by anyone who wants it.

NOTE--This story has been told me by several Mewuk Indians independently. The only variation of consequence is that, in one version, Wek'-wek and We-pi-ah'-gah gave a feast and invited the Mountain People to come; and it was while they were there that Tol'-le-loo put the Valley People to sleep with his flute and ran off with the fire. The story is called Oo'-ten-nas'-se-sa, though of course this is only a part.

WHY THE LIZARD MAN DID NOT RESTORE DEAD PEOPLE TO LIFE

OO-SOO'-MA-TE the Grizzly Bear and Hoi-ah'-ko the First People made the first Mewuk [Indian people]. When the Mewuk were made they had no hands to take hold of things. Then Pe-tā'-lit-tethe Little Lizard and Suk'-ka-de the Black Lizard gave them hands with five fingers.

When the first Mewuk [Indian] died, Suk'-ka-de the Black Lizard was sorry and set to work to bring him back to life. But Yu'-kah-loo the Meadowlark came and drove him away, saying, "Mewuk ut'-tud-dah, Mewuk tuk'-tuk-ko"--meaning, People no good, people smell.

NOTE--The Pā'-we-nan, who lived on the Sacramento and Feather Rivers from the junction of American River northward nearly to the Yuba, hold a belief which, while in some respects strikingly similar, is in other respects widely different. They say:

In the beginning Hi'-kaht the great chief said that when a person died, he should come to life on the fourth day thereafter, and should live again.

Then Hool the Meadowlark-man said No; he did not want Nis'-se-nan' [people] to live again after they were dead. He said Nis'-se-nan' were no good and by and by would smell; they had better stay dead.

Yawm the Coyote-man agreed with Hool the Meadowlark-man--he did not want people to live again; he wanted them to stay dead.

Yawm the Coyote-man had a daughter of whom he was very fond.

Hi'-kaht the great chief, after hearing Yawm say that he wanted people to stay dead after they died, went out into the brush and took a branch of a plant called Sak-ki-ak and laid it in the trail. In the night the plant turned into Koi'-maw the rattlesnake. The next morning Yawm's daughter came along the trail and Koi'-maw bit her and she died.

Yawm the Coyote-man found the dead body of his daughter and felt badly. He picked her up and said, "In four days you will come to life again."

But Hi'-kaht replied, "No, she will not come to life again. You said that when people died you wanted them to stay dead. So your daughter will stay dead and will not live again."

This is the reason why everybody stays dead after they die and nobody lives again.

THE COYOTE AND THE LIZARD

O-LA'-CHOO the Coyote-man and Pe-tā'-le the little Lizard-man made the world and everything in it.After they had done this, Pe-tā'-le wanted to turn into the Moon but O-lā'-choo the Coyote-man and Yu'-ka-loo the Meadowlark-man would not allow him to do so. [1]

---

[1] This reference to the moon is the only one I have discovered among the Mewuk creation myths. But the next people on the north--the Nissenan--count the Moon-man among the early divinities. The Southern Nissenan give the following account of the creation of man: In the beginning, Pombok the Moon-man, O'-leh the Coyote-man, and Pit-chak the Lizard-man decided to make people but differed as to what the first man should be like, for each of the three wanted man to be like himself.

After they had argued a long time they finally agreed that man should have a round face like the Moon-man, but they could not agree as to his hands. Coyote-man insisted that he should have paws like his own, but Lizard-man said that paws would be of no use-that man should have five fingers so he could take hold of things. Finally Lizard-man carried his point and gave man five long fingers like his own.

Coyote-man never forgave him, and to this day the Coyote hunts the lizard and kills him whenever he can.

HOW THE PEOPLE GOT FIVE FINGERS; HOW THEY OBTAINED FIRE; AND HOW THEY BROKE UP INTO TRIBES

ALL the world was dark.

OS-sā'-le the Coyote-man and Pe-tā'-le the Lizard-man were First People. They tried to make Indian people, each like himself. Os-sā'-le said he was going to make man just like himself.

Pe-tā'-le said that would be absurd; "How could man eat or take hold of anything if he had no fingers?"

So they quarrelled, and Os-sā'-le tried to kill Pe-tā'-le; but Pe-tā'-le slid into a crack in a rock where Os-sā'-le could not reach him. Then they talked and argued for a long time. After a while Pe-tā'-le came out ahead and when they made people he gave them five fingers.

The world was dark and everybody wanted light and fire. By and by Pe-tā'-le the Lizard said, "I see smoke down in the valley; who will go and get it. Loo'-loo-e the White-footed Mouse runs fast and plays the flute well; he had better go." So Loo'-loo-e went with his flute (loo'-lah) and found the home of the Valley People and played for them. They liked his music and gave a big feast and asked him to come into the roundhouse and play so that everyone might hear him.

We'-pi-ah'-gah the Eagle was chief of the Valley People and Wek'-wek the Falcon lived with him. When all the people had assembled and Loo'-loo-e the Mouse was there with his flute, Captain We-pi-ah'-gah took the big feather blanket called kook'-si-u, made of feathers of Mol'-luk the Condor, and closed the doorway with it and made it very tight, for he had a feeling that Loo'-loo-e might try to steal something and run off with it.

Then Loo'-loo-e took his flute and began to play; he lay on his back and rocked to and fro and played for a long time. Everyone liked the music and felt happy. In a little while they all became sleepy. Soon Loo'-loo-e looked around and saw that they were asleep; but he kept on playing till everybody was sound asleep. Then he got up and went to the fire and stole it all--two small coals--and put them in his flute and started to run away. But he could not get out of the roundhouse because of the thick feather blanket which We-pi-ah'-gah had hung over the doorway. So he stopped and cut a hole through it with his teeth and then ran out and hurried toward the mountains.

After a while the people awoke and found that the fire was gone. They were sure that Loo'-loo-e the Mouse had stolen it, and said, "Whom can we send who is fast enough to overtake him? Of all our people only Sah'-win-ne the Hail and Nuk'-kah the Shower are fast enough." So they sent these two to catch him. They rushed off toward the mountains and overtook him.

He saw them coming and put one coal in the oo'-noo tree (buckeye) and threw the other in the water. When Sah'-win-ne and Nuk'-kah caught him they could not find the coals. He told them to look, he had nothing. They looked and found nothing, and went back and told the Valley People.

Then Loo'-loo-e took the coal from the oo'noo tree and put it back in his flute and ran up into the mountains with it and gave it to his people, and they put it in the middle of the roundhouse. Before this their country was dark, and they had always eaten their food raw. Now they could see and could cook meat.

Then Os-sā'-le the Coyote-man brought the intestines of a deer and put them on the fire, covering it up and nearly putting it out. Because of his selfishness in doing this the people changed his name from Os-sā'-le to Kat'-wah (greedy), which they call him to this day.

Then the people felt cold, and only those in the middle of the roundhouse could talk as they had talked before. Those around the sides were so cold that their teeth chattered and they could not talk plainly. They separated into four groups on the four sides of the house--one on the north, one on the south, one on the east, and one on the west--and each group began to speak differently from the others, and also differently from the one in the middle. This is the way the speech of the people began to break up into five languages, and this is the way the five tribes [1] began--the people being driven apart by the selfishness of Coyote.

---

[1] The Méwah knew only five tribes: their own; the people to the north, whom they call Tam'-moo-lek or Tah-mah-lā'-ko (from Tah'-mah, north); those on the east, whom they call Mo'-nok or He'-sah-duk (from He-sum, east); those on the south, whom they call Choo'-mat-tuk (from Choo'-match, south), and those on the west, whom they call O'-loo-kuk or Ol'-lo-kuk (from O'-lo-win or Ol'-lo-win, meaning down west—in the valley).

THE BIRTH OF WEK'-WEK AND THE CREATION OF MAN

IN the beginning there was a huge bird of the vulture kind whose name was Mol'-luk, the California Condor. His home was on the mountain called Oo'-yum-bel'-le (Mount Diablo), whence he could look out over the world--westerly over San Francisco Bay and the great ocean; easterly over the tules and the broad flat Joaquin Valley.

Every morning Mol'-luk went off to hunt, and every evening he came back to roost on a large rock on the east side of the mountain. One morning he noticed that something was the matter with the rock, but did not know what the trouble was, or what to do for it. So he went off to consult the doctors. The doctors were brothers, two dark snipe-like little birds who lived on a small creek near the foot of the mountain. He told them his rock was sick and asked them to go with him, and led them to it. When they saw the rock they said, "The rock is your wife; she is going to give you a child;" and added, "we must make a big fire." Then all three set to work packing wood; they worked hard and brought a large quantity and made a big fire. Then they took hold of the rock, tore it loose, rolled it into the fire, and piled more wood around it. When the rock became hot, it burst open with a great noise, and from the inside out darted Wek'-wek the Falcon. As he came out he said 'wek' and passed on swiftly without stopping. He flew over all the country--north, south, east, and west--to see what it was like.

At that time there were no people. And there were no elderberry trees except a single one far away to the east in the place where the Sun gets up. There, in a den of rattlesnakes on a round topped hill grew lah'-pah the elderberry tree. Its branches, as they swayed in the wind, made a sweet musical sound. The tree sang; it sang all the time, day and night, and the song was good to hear. Wek'-wek looked and listened and wished he could have the tree. Near by he saw two Hol-luk'-ki or Star-people, and as he looked he perceived that they were the Hul-luk mi-yum'-ko--the great and beautiful women-chiefs of the Star-people. One was the Morning Star, the other Pleiades Os-so-so'-li. They were watching and working close by the elderberry tree. Wek'-wek liked the music and asked the Star-women about it. They told him that the tree whistled songs that kept them awake all day and all night so they could work all the time and never grow sleepy. They had the rattlesnakes to keep the birds from carrying off the elderberries.

Then Wek'-wek returned to his home on Oo-yum-bel'-le (Mount Diablo) and told Mol'-luk his father what he had seen. He said he had seen the beautiful Star-women and had heard the soft whistling song of the elderberry tree that keeps one from feeling sleepy. He asked his father how they could get the music tree and have it at their home on Oo'-yum-bel'-le.

Mol'-luk the Condor looking off over the World from his Rock on
Mount Diablo

Mol'-luk answered, "My son, I do not know; I am not very wise; you will have to ask your grandfather; he knows everything."

"Where is my grandfather?" asked Wek'-wek.

"He is by the ocean," Mol'-luk replied.

"I never saw him," said Wek'-wek.

His father asked, "Didn't you see something like a stump bobbing in the water and making a noise as it went up and down?"

"Yes," said Wek'-wek, "I saw that."

"Well," replied Mol'-luk, "that is your grandfather."

"How can I get him?" asked Wek'-wek.

"You can't get all of him, but perhaps you can break off a little piece and in that way get him."

So Wek'-wek flew off to the ocean, found the stump bobbing in the water, and tore off a little piece and brought it home. When he awoke next morning the little piece had changed into O-let'-te, the Coyote-man, who was already living in a little house of his own on top of the mountain. O-let'-te told Wek'-wek that he was his grandfather.

Wek'-wek told Mol'-luk his father and added, "Now I've got my grandfather." Mol'-luk replied, "Ask him what you want to know; he knows everything."

So Wek'-wek asked O-let'-te, "How are we going to get the elderberry music?"

"Ho-ho," answered O-let'-te, "that is very difficult; you might have bad luck and might be killed."

But Wek'-wek continued, "I want it."

Then the wise O-let'-te said: "All right, go and buy it, but mind what I tell you or you will be killed. You will find the Star-women pleasant and pretty. They will want you to stay and play with them. If you do so, you will die. Go and do as I tell you."

So Wek'-wek went. He flew fast and far--far away to the east, to the place where the Sun gets up. There he found Hul-luk mi-yum'-ko the Star-women and lah'-pah the elderberry tree. The Star-women were people of importance; both were chiefs. Wek'-wek had taken with him long strings of haw'-wut, the shell money, which as he flew streamed out behind. This he gave them for the elderberry music. The Star-women liked the haw'-wut and accepted it and led Wek'wek to the elderberry tree and told him to break off a little piece and take it home and he would have all. But when he reached the tree the rattlesnakes stood up all around and hissed at him to frighten him, for he was a stranger. The Star-women told him not to be afraid, they would drive the snakes away. So they scolded the snakes and sent them down into their holes. Then Wek'-wek took his soo'-pe [digging stick] and pried off a piece of the tree. The Star-women began to play with him and wanted him to stay with them, but remembering what O-let'-te his grandfather had told him, he paid no attention to them but took the piece of elderberry tree and carried it swiftly home to Oo-yum-bel'le.

When he arrived he said to O-let'-te, "Grandfather, I've brought the music-tree; what shall we do with it so we can have the music?"

O-let'-te laughed as he replied, "Do you really think you have it?"

"Yes," answered Wek'-wek, "here it is."

Then O-let'-te said, "We must put it in the ground over all the country to furnish music for the Mew'-ko [Indian people] we are going to make, for pretty soon we shall begin to make the people."

Wek'-wek answered "Yes," but thought he would wait and see who was the smarter, himself or O-let'-te-for he felt very proud because he had brought the music tree.

Then they went out and traveled over' all the country and planted the elderberry tree so that by and by it would furnish music and food and medicine for the Indian people they were going to make. O-let'-te told Wek'-wek that the berries would make food, the roots and blossoms medicine, and the hollow branches music.

KE'-LOK AND HIS HAN-NA'-BOO

WHEN Wek'-wek and O-let'-te were out hunting one day they went to Tah-lah'-wit the North and came to a rocky hill where they saw a great and powerful giant named Ke'-lok, sitting by his han-nā'-boo or roundhouse. Wek'-wek flew close to him and saw him well.

That night, when they had gone home, Wek'-wek said to O-let'-te, "Grandfather, I want to play al'-leh (the hand-game) with Ke'-lok." [1]

When O-let'-te heard Wek'-wek say he wanted to play al'-leh with Ke'-lok he laughed and said,

"You! play hand-game with the Giant Ke'-lok!"

"Yes," answered Wek'-wek, "I want to play hand-game with Ke'-lok."

Then his grandfather told him that Ke'-lok was his elder brother.

"All right," said Wek'-wek, "I'm going to play al'-leh with my brother."

After a while Wek'-wek arrived at Ke'-lok's han-nā'-boo, and when Ke'-lok came out, said to him, "Brother, I have come to play hand-game with you." "All right," answered Ke'-lok, and he at once built a fire and put eight round rocks in it and heated them until they were red hot. Then he said, "My young brother, you begin first."

"No," replied Wek'-wek, "I want to see you play first; you begin."

"All right," said Ke'-lok, and he immediately sprang up and darted up into the sky, for he was great and powerful and could do all things. As he went up he made a loud noise. Then he came down in a zig-zag course, and as he came, sang a song.

------

[1] Nowadays al'-leh is a guessing game, played with two small bones, one wrapped or 'dressed' to distinguish it from the other. But in those days it was different, for al'-leh was played by hurling rocks with intent to kill.

Then Wek'-wek began to throw hot rocks at him but purposely missed him, for he did not want to kill his brother. His grandfather O-let'-te the Coyote-man, called out to him from the south that if he hit Ke'-lok in his body it would not kill him, but that his heart (wus'-ke) was in his arm, under a white spot on the underside of the arm, and that if he hit that spot it would kill him; that was the only place on his body where a blow would kill him.

Wek'-wek answered, "I can easily hit that, but I don't want to kill him."

So he threw all the hot stones but took care not to hit the white spot under the arm. When he had fired all the rocks he picked them up and put them back in the fire to heat again.

Then it was Ke'-lok's turn.

The Giant Ke'-lok hurling hot Rocks at Wek'-wek

When Ke'-lok was ready, Wek'-wek said, "All right, I will go now," and he shot up into the sky, making a great noise, just as Ke'-lok had done. Then he came down slowly, singing a song, and came toward Ke'-lok's round-house.

Then Ke'-lok began to throw the hot rocks at him and tried hard to hit him. But Wek'-wek dodged them easily and called out to O-let'-te his grandfather: "He can't hit me unless I let him; see me let him hit me"--for he thought he would not really be killed, believing that the magic of O-let'-te would keep him alive. So he let Ke'-lok hit him with the last rock.

Ke'-lok did hit him and he fell dead. Then Ke'-lok picked him up and hung him on his ha-nā'-boo.

Ke'-lok's place was at Tah-lah'-wit, the north. When Wek'-wek set out to go there, his grandfather O-let'-te had told him to pluck out and take with him one of his father's long wing-feathers and stand it up on top of Ke'-lok's han-nā'-boo so it could be seen a long way off. O-let'-te said the feather would stand so long as Wek'wek was alive, but if he was killed it would fall. While the hand-game was going on O-let'-te watched the feather, and when Wek'-wek was hit he saw it fall. Then he felt very sad and cried and told Mol'-luk, Wek'-wek's father, and they both mourned and cried.

Then O-let'-te said to Mol'-luk, "I'm going to play hand-game with Ke'-lok." So he took a long walking stick with a sharp point at one end and set out on the far journey to Tah-lah'-wit. When he arrived at Ke'lok's han-nā'-boo he said, "Well, how are you getting along?"

Ke'-lok answered, "I'm getting along all right."

Then O-let'-te said, "I have come to play hand-game."

"All right," replied Ke'-lok; and he built a fire and heated the rocks red hot, just as he had done before. When the rocks were hot he asked, "Who will play first?"

O-let'-te answered, "I'm an old man, but I'll go first." So he shot up into the sky with a great noise, just as Ke'-lok and Wek'-wek had done before; and then circled around and came down slowly, singing a song of his own--different from the songs the others had sung.

Then Ke'-lok began picking up the hot rocks and throwing them at him. But O-let'-te, in spite of his age, was very agile and dodged all of the eight rocks so that not one hit him.

When Ke'-lok had fired all the rocks he said to himself, "Maybe my grandfather will beat me after all; I feel now that I am done for," and he was afraid.

O-let'-te, who was still in the air, then came down and said, "I'm old and tired of playing that way. Do you think old people can beat young people? I don't know, but I'll try anyhow."

It was now Ke'-lok's turn to go up and O-let'-te's turn to throw the hot rocks. Ke'-lok sprang up in the same way as before, and came down in the same way, singing his own song. O-let'-te picked up the hot stones and threw them at Ke'-lok, one after the other, until he had thrown four, but did not try to hit him. He then looked toward Ke'-lok's han-nā'-boo and saw Wek'-wek hanging there, and was very angry. When he picked up the fifth stone he said, "Now I am going to hit the white spot on his arm, over his heart," and he fired the rock straight and hit the white spot, and Ke'-lok fell dead.

As soon as Ke'-lok was dead his fire sprang up and began to burn and spread. Then O-let'-te went to Wek'-wek and took him in his hands. Wek'-wek's feathers moved a little; then his head drew in a little; then his eyes opened and he stood up and came to life and exclaimed, "The country is burning!"

And so it was, for the fire was now sweeping fiercely over the land, spreading swiftly to the east and west and south, roaring with a mighty roar, consuming everything in its way and filling the air with flame and smoke.

O-let'-te directed Wek'-wek to fly quickly to the ocean and dive under the water, where he had two sisters named Hoo-soo'-pe [1] (the Mermaids), and stay with them while the world was burning. So Wek'-wek went into the ocean and found his sisters and remained with them until the fire had

---

[1] See the story of Ho-hā'-pe, page 134.

burnt over all the land and had burnt itself out. While with them he killed a great many ducks. His sisters did not like him to kill ducks, so after they had spoken to him he killed only what he needed to eat.

THE CREATION OF MAN

AFTER a while the world cooled off and Wek'-wek came back to Oo'-yum-bel'-le (Mount Diablo) to see his father Mol'-luk and his grandfather O-let'te. He said to Mol'-luk, "O father;" and Mol'-luk answered, "What is it my son?"

Wek'-wek asked, "How can we make Mew'-ko (Indian people) and have them in the country?"

His father replied, "I cannot tell you; ask your grandfather, he can tell you."

So Wek'-wek asked his grandfather, O-let'-te, how they were going to make people.

O-let'-te answered, "Hah-hah, it will take you a good while to do that. If you are going to do that you must have a head. If people are coming you must first put out [provide] everything everywhere so they can live. If you want to do this I will think about it."

"I want to see it done," answered Wek'-wek.

"All right," said O-let'-te, "I know how. I must catch the three birds--Choo'-hoo the Turkey Buzzard, Kok'-kol the Raven, and Ah-wet'-che the Crow. The only way to catch these birds is to make-believe dead."

So Wek'-wek and O-let'-te went out on the plain together and O-let'-te lay down on the ground and pretended he was dead. He opened his mouth and let his tongue out and relaxed himself so Choo'-hoo the Buzzard would think he was dead. He told Wek'-wek he would call if he caught the birds; and Wek'-wek went away.

Soon Choo'-hoo the Turkey Buzzard came sailing over and saw the dead Coyote-man and circled around and lit on the ground beside him. Kok'-kol the Raven and Ah-wet'-che the Crow saw Choo'-hoo go down and knew that he had found something to eat, so they too hastened to the place. just as all three began to eat, O-let'-te suddenly sprang up and caught them. He then called Wek'-wek to come, and told him to pick off the feathers and be careful not to lose a single one. This Wek'-wek did; he picked all the feathers from the three birds and. took them all home.

Then he asked his grandfather, "What are we going to do next?"

"Make people," answered O-let'-te.

"All right," said Wek'-wek, "do you know how?"

"Yes," answered O-let'-te.

Wek'-wek then told Mol'-luk his father that they were going to make people. Mol'-luk answered, "All right."

Next morning O-let'-te and Wek'-wek took the feathers and traveled over all the country. They picked out the places where they wanted Indian villages to be, and in each place stuck up three feathers--one for Chā'-kah the Chief, one for Mi'-yum, the head woman or Woman Chief, and one for Soo-lā-too the poor. And they gave each place its name--the name it has always had and bears today.

The next morning the three feathers at each place stood up and came to life and became Mew'-ko [Indian People]. This is the way people were made in the beginning and this is the way all the different rancherias or villages were named.

After that O-let'-te said to Wek'-wek, "Now we also are going to change; I am going to be a hunting animal and you are going to be a hunting bird." So O-let'-te the Coyote-man, whose form up to this time we do not know, changed to the Coyote, a furry hunting animal and became the first furry animal. And Wek'-wek changed to the Falcon, a hunting bird.

HOW THEY GOT THE FIRE

THE first fire was made by the Doctor Birds at the birth of Wek'-wek. The next fire was made by Ke'-lok the North Giant. After Ke'-lok's death and after his fire had burnt up the world and had burnt itself out, there was no fire except that of the Hul-luk mi-yum'-ko, the Star-women, which was close by the elderberry tree, way off in the east where the Sun gets up.

O-let'-te said to his grandson, Wek'-wek: "Now we have people, and elderberry music for the people, but we have no fire for them to cook with; the Star-women have it; we must steal it."

"How?" asked Wek'-wek.

"Send Koo-loo'-loo the Humming-bird; he is faster than you. Tell him to catch a little spark and bring it quickly," replied O-let'-te.

"All right," answered Wek'-wek, and he sent Koo-loo'-loo to fetch the fire. Koo-loo'-loo shot out swiftly and soon reached the Star-women by the elderberry tree in the far east, in the place where the Sun gets up. Here he hid and watched and waited, and when he saw a little spark of fire, he darted in and seized it and brought it back quickly to Wek'-wek and O-let'-te. He held it tight under his chin, and to this day if you look under the Humming-bird's chin you will see the mark of the fire.

Then Wek'-wek asked: "Where shall we put it?"

O-let'-te answered, "Let us put it in oo'-noo, the buckeye tree, where all the people can get it." So they put it in oo'-noo, the buckeye tree, and even now whenever an Indian wants fire he goes to the oo'-noo tree and gets it.

FRAGMENT OF A HOO'-KOO-E'-KO VERSION

I have discovered fragments of a similar myth among the nearly extinct Hoo'-koo-e'-ko north of San Francisco Bay. These people state that O'-ye the Coyote-man sent Koo-loo'-pis the Hummingbird far away to the east to steal the fire; that he brought it back to Coyote-man, and that Coyote-man put it into the buckeye tree. They state also that Wek'-wek once went a long way off and was killed, and that his grandfather, O'-ye the Coyote-man, went after him and restored him to life.

HOW KAH'-KOOL THE RAVEN BECAME A GREAT HUNTER

A LONG time ago Too'-le the Evening Star lived at Oo'-tin [Bower Cave, on the Coulterville road to Yosemite]. He-le'-jah the Mountain Lion lived with him. They were chiefs and partners and had a room on the north side of the cave. There were other people here also To-lo'-mah the Wild Cat, Yu'-wel the Gray Fox, Kah'-kool the Raven, and many more.

They used to send out hunters for meat. One of these, Kah'-kool the Raven, complained to Too'-le and He-le'-jah that he could not come near enough the game to shoot; the animals saw him too easily--he was too light colored. So he decided to make himself black; he took some charcoal and mashed it in a basket and rubbed it all over his body wherever he could reach, and had the others help put it on his back where he could not reach. When he was black all over he went hunting and killed two or three animals the first day, for now they could not see him.

One day Kah'-kool went to Big Meadows and climbed on top of Pile Peak, and when the moon rose, he saw away in the east two big things like ears standing up. He had never seen anything like them before and ran back to Oo'-tin and told the Chiefs. He said the animal must be very big and very wild, for it turned its big ears every way. He wanted to see it.

Every evening he went back to the peak and saw the ears in the east, and each time they were a little nearer. But he did not yet know what the animal was. Then he went again and this time the ears were only two or three miles away, and he ran back quickly and told the Chiefs that the new animals were coming. They were Deer coming over the mountains from the east; they had never been here before.

The next morning Kah'-kool went out and for the first time in his life saw a bunch of Deer; but he did not know what they were. He saw that they stepped quickly, and that some of them had horns. So he ran back and told

Too'-le and He-le'-jah what he had seen, and said that the new animals looked good to eat and he wanted to kill one.

"All right, "answered the Chiefs, "If you see one on our side [1] go ahead and kill him."

So the next morning Kah'-kool again went out and saw that the animals had come much nearer and were pretty close. He hid behind a tree and they came still nearer. He picked out a big one and shot his arrow into it and killed it, for he wanted to try the meat. He watched it kick and roll over and die, and then went back and told the Chiefs that he had killed one and wanted two men to go with him and fetch it. The Chiefs sent two men with him, but when they got there they had nothing to cut it with and had to carry it home whole. One took it by the front feet, the other by the hind feet; they carried it to the cave and showed it to the Chiefs.

Kah'-kool the Raven-Hunter bringing in his first Deer. "He-le'-jah said it was a Deer and was good to eat."

---

[1] Meaning "on our side" of the tribal boundary line. This line now separates the territory of the Middle Mewuk from that of the Mono Lake Piutes.

He-le'-jah said it was a Deer and was good to eat, and told the people to skin it. They did so and ate it all at one meal.

Next morning Kah'-kool returned alone to the same place and followed the tracks and soon found the Deer. He hid behind a tree and shot one. The others ran, but he shot his arrows so quickly that they made only a few jumps before he had killed five--enough for all the people. He did not want to kill all; he wanted to leave some bucks and does so there would be more.

This time the Chiefs sent five men with Kah'-kool. They took flint knives and skinned the Deer and carried home all the meat and intestines for supper and breakfast.

Chief Too'-le the Evening Star told Kah'-kool that he wanted to see how the Deer walked, and would hunt with him. Kah'-kool replied that he was too light--too shiny--and would scare the Deer. Too'-le said he would hide behind a tree and not show himself. So he went, and Kah'-kool kept him behind. But he was so bright that the Deer saw him and ran away. Too'-le said, "What am I going to do?" Kah'-kool made no answer; he was angry because he had to go home without any meat.

Next morning Too'-le went again. He said he was smart and knew what he would do. The Deer had now made a trail. Too'-le dug a hole by the trail and covered himself up with leaves and thought that when the Deer came he would catch one by the foot. But when the Deer came they saw his eye shine and ran away.

The next morning he tried again. He said that this time he would bury himself eye and all, and catch a Deer by the foot. Kah'-kool answered, "You can't catch one that way, you will have to shoot him." But Too'-le dug a hole in another place in the trail and covered himself all up, eye and all, except the tips of his fingers. The Deer came and saw the tips of his fingers shine and ran away. So again the hunters had to go back without any meat.

Then Too'-le the Evening Star said, "I'm going to black myself with charcoal, the same as Kah'-kool did." He tried, but the charcoal would not stick--he was too bright. He said, "I don't know what to do; I want to kill one or two Deer." Then he tried again and mashed more charcoal and put it on thick. The others helped him and finally made him black all over. Too'-le did not know that the Deer could smell him, and again hid on the trail. The Deer came again. This time the doe was ahead, the buck behind. The leader, the doe, smelled him and jumped over him; the buck smelled him and ran back. So this time also Too'-le and Kah'-kool had to go home without meat.

The next morning Too'-le tried once more. He had two men blacken him all over. Then he went to the trail and stood still between two trees. But the Deer smelled him and swung around and ran away and went down west to the low country. This discouraged him so that he did not know what to do, and he gave up hunting and stayed at home.

Then Kah'-kool began to hunt again; he went every morning alone and killed five or ten Deer. The people ate the meat and intestines and all, but did not have enough. Then Kah'-kool worked harder; he started very early in the morning, before daylight, and killed twelve to fifteen Deer every day. This was too much for him and before long he took sick and could not hunt at all.

Then the Chiefs and all the others had nothing to eat and did not know what to do. Too'-le asked He-le'-jah, and He-le'-jah asked Too'-le, what they should do. He-le'-jah said he would stay and kill his own Deer and eat the liver only--not the meat--and would eat it raw. Too'-le said he would go up into the sky and stay there and become the Evening Star. And each did as he had said. So the rancheria at Oo'-tin was broken up.

HOW KAH'-KAH-LOO THE RAVENS BECAME PEOPLE

WHEN water covered the world only the top of the highest mountain rose above it. The people had climbed up on this mountain, but could find no food and were starving. They wanted to go off and get something to eat. When the water went down all the ground was soft mud. After a while the people rolled rocks down to see if the mud were hard enough to hold them. When the rocks stayed on top, the people went down to search for food.

But the mud was not hard enough to hold them and they sank out of sight, leaving deep holes where they had gone down. Then Kah'-kah-loo the Ravens came and stood at the holes, one at each hole where a man had gone down. After a while, when the ground hardened, the Ravens turned into people. That is the reason the Mewuk are so dark.

THE BEAR AND THE FAWNS

OO-SOO'-MA-TE the Grizzly Bear had a sister-in-law whose name was O-woo'-yah the Deer. Oo-soo'-ma-te took her to a place in the woods to show her a good kind of clover. When they found it O-woo'-yah began to scratch her head. Oo-soo'-ma-te said, "Let me look in your head," and seized her by the neck and killed her, and took her liver out and put it in a basket and carried it home.

O-woo'-yah the Deer was the mother of two little fawns, brothers, and Oo-soo'-ma-te was the mother of a little boy--a little bear cub.

When Oo-soo'-ma-te came home with the liver in her basket the little fawns asked, "Aunt, where is our mother?"

The Bear replied, "She is out gathering clover."

After a little they asked, "Why doesn't mother come home?" Then they saw the liver in the basket and smelled it and knew it was their mother's liver. Then they began to cry and say, "Our mother is dead, our mother is dead."

Old Oo-soo'-ma-te was outside pounding acorns. The little fawns went out and asked if they might take her baby and play with it.

She answered, "All right, but don't hurt him." So they took the baby bear out in the woods to play, and went to the side of a hill and dug a hole. They said to the cub, "We will go in first and you close the hole and smoke us, and when we call, you let us out. Then you go in and we will smoke you."

So they went in first and the baby bear closed the hole and made smoke go in, and when the smoke was thick the fawns called to be let out, and the cub let them out. Then the cub went in and the fawns closed the hole and made smoke go in. The cub said, "When I call, you let me out," and the fawns answered, "All right." But when the bear cub called to be let out the fawns poked more leaves and pine needles into the hole and made more smoke, and the little bear kept crying till he died. After he was dead they took him out.

Then they said, "What shall we do? What shall we tell our Aunt?"

Just then Oo-soo'-ma-te, who was still pounding acorns, called them to come home.

The fawns laid the baby bear on the ground near the house so their Aunt could see it, and told her it was asleep and they were going to play again.

She answered, "Don't go far, your mother will be here pretty soon."

The little brothers then ran off to the south as fast as they could go, so Oo-soo'-ma-te could not find them. Every time they passed a tree on the trail they peeled a little bark off and spat on the place and told it to call out when Oo-soo'-ma-te came looking for them. This they did to all the trees till they came to a big river with a high hill on the far side; then they crossed the river and climbed up the hill.

The Fawns asking the Mother Bear if they may play with her Baby

Soon the trees began to shout and the fawns knew that Oo-soo'-ma-te was coming, and after a while they saw her coming. She saw them on the far side of the river and asked how they had crossed. They told her to turn her head the other way and walk backward. Then they quickly made a hot fire and heated two big rocks with hard white chunks in them.

When Oo-soo'-ma-te was nearly across the river the older fawn went to the edge of the water and knelt down, and the younger one rolled a hot rock, which just missed his brother's knee. The older one then ran up to the fire and said, "Let me do that and you kneel down." And he took the other big hot rock, and rolled it down the hill. It grazed his brother's knee a little and then hit the old bear and she fell back in the river and was drowned.

Then the fawns began to wonder what they had better do. First they dragged the old bear out of the water and cut her hide on the back and made a long rope of it and took the rope with them. Then the younger one asked, "Where are we going now? Up east?"

"No," answered the elder one. "Where then, going north?" "No."

"Going west?" "No." "Where then, south?" "No."

"Then where are we going, up in the sky?" asked the little one.

"No," replied the other.

"Are we going under the earth?" "Yes," said the elder brother.

Then the younger one said, "You don't know where we are going; ask me." And the elder brother asked the younger, "Are we going north?" "No," was the reply.

"West?" "No."

"South?" "No."

"Where then, under the earth?" "No."

"Where do you want to go--up in the sky?"

"Yes," answered the younger; so they went up in the sky and there they found their mother.

She was glad to see her boys. They said, "We are thirsty; where is the water?" She answered, "I have no water here, I'll go to the spring to get it." And she went to the spring and fell in and was drowned. Then the brothers let themselves down with the rope they had made from the hide of the Mother Bear, and came back to this world. If their mother had not drowned, the fawns would have stayed up there and there would be no deer here on the earth.

THE BEAR AND THE FAWNS

A story sung by the Middle Mewuk

OO-SOO'-MA-TE the Grizzly Bear killed Ut-too'-yah the Mother Deer. Oo-soo'-ma-te killed her and He-le'-jah the Mountain Lion ate her. The Mother Deer had two little fawns. They missed their mother--and asked Oo-soo'-ma-te where she was. Oo-soo'-ma-te answered, "She is resting," and pointing to the house said, "Go in there where you will be safe till she comes back."

They went in, singing for their mother to come back, for they were starving. When they were inside, Oo-soo'-ma-te closed the door so they could not get out.

Then the fawns felt sure that Oo-soo'-ma-te had killed their mother and was intending to kill them. So they fastened the door of the Bear's house on the inside so she could not get in. Then a kind one--Te-wi'-yu the Red-shafted Flicker--brought them fire and they put it in the middle of the house and put on a number of rocks to heat.

When Oo-soo'-ma-te came home she was unable to get in and called to the fawns, saying, "I want to come in; where is the door?"

They answered, "Try the west side."

She tried, but could not find any door.

Then they called to her to try the north side, and she did so, but could not find it.

Then they told her to try the cast side, and she did, with no better success; then the south side, with the same result.

This made Oo-soo'-ma-te very angry and she shouted, "If you don't open the door and let me in I'll come and eat you."

Then they told her to climb up on top and come in through the smoke hole, and to back down or she would fall and break her neck.

So she climbed up on top and began to back down through the smoke hole. But by this time the rocks were hot, and while she was trying to squeeze through the hole the fawns took the hot rocks and burned her to death.

HOW THE CHILDREN OF HE-LE'-JAH BECAME PEOPLE

HE-LE'-JAH the Cougar or Mountain Lion had two wives, Oo-soo'-ma-te the Grizzly Bear-woman and Paht'-ki-yu the Raccoon-woman. Their children looked a little like people but still were not people.Every year there were more children, and as they grew up and had children of their own, the children came to look more and more like people, only they had no fingers.

Then Pe-tā'-le the Lizard gave them five fingers and they became real people (Me'wuk).

THE GREED OF HIS'-SIK THE SKUNK

HIS'-SIK the Skunk had a wife, and by and by a daughter, who, when she grew up, married Yu'-wel the Gray Fox. Yu'-wel was a good hunter and he and His'-sik often hunted together.

Not far from His'-sik's place were two high hills standing side by side. In the narrow gap between them ran the trail of So'-koi the Elk. One day His'-sik told Yu'-wel to hide in this narrow place while he went down to the plain to drive up the elk. So Yu'-wel hid there and His'-sik went down near the elk and fired his terrible scent. The elk could not stand the smell and ran up the trail. Yu'-wel waited until the leader and all the others had passed up between the hills, and when the last one had gone by he stepped behind him and fired his arrow with such force that it shot through the whole band, killing them all.

When His'-sik came he was so glad that he danced. He called all the people to come and help carry the meat home; and then said to Yu'-wel: "You must pack one elk and pack me too, for I am too tired to walk."

Yu'-wel was afraid of His'-sik and so did as he was told. He lifted a big elk on his shoulders, and His'-sik climbed up on top, and while they were on the way danced all the time on the body of the elk, and Yu'-wel carried them both to the village.

Then His'-sik told the people to skin the elk, and promised them some of the meat. They skinned the elk and cut the meat in strips and hung it up to dry. When they had done this they asked him for their share. He refused to give them any but told them that they might eat acorn mush and pinole. He then turned as if he were going to shoot his scent, and everyone was afraid.

His'-sik was so greedy that he would not give any of the meat to anyone--not even to his own wife and daughter, nor to his son-in-law who killed it--but put it all away to dry for himself.

The next day he told Yu'-wel to hunt again, and they did the same as before; and when the elk were in the narrow pass between the hills Yu'-wel shot his arrow and killed the whole bunch, as before.

Then His'-sik called the people to come and carry the elk home, and made Yu'-wel carry one, and he danced on top on the way, as before.

Again he told the people to skin the elk and he would give them meat for supper; but when they had skinned the elk and cut up the meat he told them to eat acorns and pinole, at the same time turning to frighten them, and took all the meat to dry for himself, just as he had done before. The people were very angry, but were afraid to do anything for fear His'-sik would shoot his scent and kill them. They talked the matter over for a long time and finally a wise man said: "What are we going to do? Must we hunt for him and pack his meat and skin it for him always, and not get any? We had better kill him, but how can we do it so he will not shoot his scent and kill us?"

Then Too'-wik the Badger spoke. He said, "We can kill him." And while His'-sik was watching his meat so no one could take any of it, Too'-wik dug a big hole, ten or fifteen feet deep, and built a fire in it.

Someone asked him why he made the fire. Too'-wik replied, "Do you not know that His'-sik is a great dancer and loves to dance? We will have fire in the hole, and cover the top over with sticks and leaves and earth so he can't see anything, and send for him to come and dance, and when he dances he will break through and fall in and we shall kill him."

The people answered, "All right."

When it was dark they sent a messenger to His'-sik. He said, "You are a great dancer; we want a dance tonight and will pay you well if you will come.")

His'-sik was pleased and answered, "All right, where shall I dance?"

They took him to the place and pointing to it said, "Right here."

His'-sik began to dance and sing, and everyone said, "Good, you are doing well; keep on, you are doing finely; go ahead, you surely are a great dancer." And they flattered him and he kept on and danced harder and harder, for he was proud and wanted to show what he could do.

After a while, when he was dancing hardest, the sticks broke and he fell into the hole. The people were ready. They had a big rock, a very big rock, which it had taken many people to bring. They were waiting, and the moment he fell in they pushed the rock quickly over the hole and held it down; they all climbed up on it and held it down tight so he could not get out.

The hot coals burnt his feet and made him dance. He was very angry and shot his scent so hard against the side of the hole that he pushed mountains up on that side; then he turned the other way and shot again and pushed mountains up on that side too. After this his scent was gone and the coals burnt him and killed him. Then all the people were happy.

The next day the people had a great feast and ate all the dried meat they wanted.

NEK'-NA-KA'-TAH THE ROCK MAIDEN

Ancient Mortar-holes in the Granite Rock

IN the mountains among the rocks by the river lives Nek'-na-kā'-tah, the little rock girl. She is herself a rock and always lives in rocky places by the river. In some way she produces or gives off people; these people are hard like rocks and you can not cut them or shoot them with an arrow.

A long time ago Oo-soo'-ma-te the Grizzly Bear and Hoi-yah'-ko the FIRST PEOPLE, made the Chaw'-se or mortar holes in the big flat-topped rocks. Then Nek'-na-kā'-tah the rock maiden came and helped make the Kah-wah'-che or stone pestles for the people to pound acorns with.

THE JEALOUSY OF WEK'-WEK AND THE DEATH OF LO'-WUT

WEK'-WEK the Falcon-man was Chief and Captain of all the bird-people. He used to hunt birds for food and also used to catch birds alive to bring back to his han-nā'-boo (roundhouse) where he kept them locked up until he could turn them into people. O-lā'-nah the Coyote-man stood guard at the door of the han-nā'-boo.

Wek'-wek the Falcon-man and Ho'-pah the White-headed Eagle-man had the power to make people out of birds. For this reason they were jealous of one another. Besides, Ho'-pah was in love with Wek'-wek's wife, Lo'-wut, the Gray Goose-woman. So Wek'-wek had cause to be jealous.

Once when he went out to go hunting he hid and watched and saw Ho'-pah and Lo'-wut together. This made him very angry. When he came back he asked Lo'-wut, his wife, "Have you anything ready to eat? I'm hungry."

"Yes," she replied.

"Bring me some water first," he said, "I'm thirsty; bring good water; don't get it from the edge of the river; go out where it is deep and get it there."

Lo'-wut did as she was told and came back with good clear water, but when she reached the house with it, it had turned into snakes and frogs and other water animals. [1] Five times she went out into the river for water, each time with the same result. The last time she waded out till the water was above her waist.

While she was gone, Wek'-wek went to her bed and fixed in it four long spear points of flint with the points up. When she came the fifth time with snakes and frogs instead of water, Wek'-wek seized her and threw her down on the bed and the four spear points pierced her body and killed her.

---

[1] Wek'-wek made this happen, for he was a magician or witch doctor.

To-to'-kol the Sandhill Crane-woman was Lo'wut's mother; she was very angry because Wek'wek had killed her daughter, and wanted to punish him.

O-lā'-nah the Coyote-man and Soo'-choo-koo the Spoon-bill Duck came to carry Lo'wut's dead body to the han-nā'-boo, but when they lifted it they saw on the breast the black marks which Ho'-pah her lover had painted there. Wek'-wek had seen these before and knew. So O-lā'-nah and Soo'-choo-koo took the dead body and buried it.

When Lo'-wut died she left two children, a baby and a little boy. Their grandmother, To-to'-kol, took care of them and every day sent the little boy with the baby to the roundhouse to be fed--and for four days Lo'-wut the dead mother came each day to the han-nā'-boo to give milk to her young child.

Funeral of Lo'-wuk, wife of Wek'-wek

On the fourth day Wek'-wek asked his little boy where he went every day with the little one. The boy, afraid to tell the truth, said he took the child to give it milk of the milkweed plant.

Wek'-wek hid in the top of an oak tree and watched. He saw his dead wife Lo'-wut come to the roundhouse to give breast to the child; and saw her rise from the ground and shake the earth of the grave out of her hair.

Then Wek'-wek found that he loved her still, although she had been unfaithful to him. So he went into the roundhouse and caught her in his arms and hugged her.

"Let me go," she said, "You can't get me back; I'm not well as I used to be."

"That doesn't make any difference," he said, "I'll cure you." And he took her away to his own roundhouse, where the other bird-people were. It was dark when they arrived.

Yu-koo'-le the Meadowlark was there. He had never liked Wek'-wek's wife and had quarrelled with her. Now he made a great fuss and noise.

"Hoo," he said, "light a light; I smell something like a dead body."

At that very moment Wek'-wek was sitting in the middle of the roundhouse holding the body of his wife, whom he was bringing back to life. But when Yu-koo'-le spoke and said what he did, the dead woman disappeared.

Wek'-wek was very angry. He spoke and said to the rest of the birds (all of whom were going to be people): "This now is the way it will be with us all. When we die we shall die forever. Had it not been for Yu-koo'-le we would live again after the fourth day and be alive forever, the same as before."

When Wek'-wek had said this he seized Yu-koo'-le and tore his mouth open and killed him, and to this day you can see under the meadowlark's throat the black mark where his mouth was torn down, and the marks on his head where the skull was crushed.

Then Wek'-wek sent all the bird-people away, but before they went he spoke to them and said: "Now you will never be people but will be real birds; if Yu-koo'-le had not said what he did my wife would have lived and all of you would have turned into people."

All the bird-people in the roundhouse were angry at what Yu-koo'-le had done. They said, "Were it not for Yu-koo'-le we would turn into people;

now we must turn into animals." Then they came out of the roundhouse, one at a time, and as each came out it sang the song of the kind of bird it was to be, and became that kind, and went away.

THE DEFEAT OF O-LA'-NAH THE COYOTE-MAN

WEK'-WEK the Falcon-man and O-lā'-nah the Coyote-man lived a long time ago.

Wek'-wek did not like O-lā'-nah because he was smart and always pretended that he could do everything. So one day Wek'-wek said to him, "Let's go and get wood; you are so smart and know so much and can do so many things, let's see you take that big oak tree and bring it home."

O-lā'-nah answered, "All right, I can do it."

Wek'-wek told him to go ahead and do it.

Then O-lā'-nah ran around and around the big oak tree and the roots cracked and made a noise, and the tree shook, but it did not fall; O-lā'-nah could not get it up; he made it shake four times but could not make it fall.

Wek'-wek, who was watching from the top of a sycamore tree, said, "Do that again; make the big oak tree shake again, the same as you did before, you are so strong."

O-lā'-nah tried but could not do it.

Then Wek'-wek said: "What you said was not true; you bragged that you could do everything but you can not do any thing; now I have beaten you, haven't I?"

"Yes," answered O-lā'-nah, "You have beaten me; I am going away." Then O-lā'-nah turned and howled as Coyotes howl and cried and said "how-loo'-loo-e, how-loo'-loo-e, how-loo'-loo-e," and turned into a real Coyote like the coyotes we have now. But he was angry and set upon O-hul'-le, his wife (O-hul'-le was the Badger-woman), and whipped her, and she ran away. O-lā'-nah followed and tried to hiring her back, but she refused and would not come.

After Wek'-wek had beaten O-lā'-nah he had to get fire. So he went up the Sacramento River to the place where trees grow, where the creeks come down from the mountains, and took a piece of wood and made a small hole in it and sprinkled in the hole some dry leaves of Kutch'-um the sage-herb, and took a stick of Lap'-pah, the elderberry tree, and whirled it between his hands, with one end in the hole in the wood, and fire came in the dry Kutch'-um leaves and he had fire.

HOW SAH'-TE SET THE WORLD ON FIRE

A LONG time ago, before there were any than people, Ol'-le the Coyote-man and his grandson, Wek'-wek the Falcon, lived together at Tu'-le-yo'-me. In those days Wek'-wek hunted Hoo-yu'-mah the Meadowlark and ate no other game, and Ol'-le the Coyote-man ate nothing at all.

One day Wek'-wek said: "Grandfather, I want to see what is on the other side of Mel'-le-a-loo'-mah. [1] I want to see the country on the other side."

"All right," answered Ol'-le.

So the next morning Wek'-wek set out and crossed over the Mel'-le-a-loo'-mah hills to Coyote Valley, and a little farther on came to a small lake called Wen'-nok pol'-pol, at the south end of which was a pretty pointed mountain called Loo-peek'-pow-we. On the lake were great numbers of ducks and geese. Up to this time he had never killed any of these-he had killed only Hoo-yu'-mah the Meadowlark.

He went back to Tu'-le-yo'-me, and told his grandfather what he had seen, and asked how he could get the ducks and geese. His grandfather answered: "A long time ago my father taught me how to make low'-ke the sling, and how to put loo'-poo the small stone in it, and how to aim and fire by swinging it around and letting fly." Then Ol'-le took kol the tule and made a low'-ke of it for Wek'-wek. The next morning Wek'-wek took the low'-ke and loo'-poo and went back to Wen'-nok-pol'-pol, the little lake, and stood on top of Loo-peek'-pow-we the sharp-pointed mountain at the south end of the lake, from which he could see over all the valley. The flat ground at the base of the mountain was covered with geese of the black-neck kind called Lah'-kah. At the foot of the peak was a small flat-topped

---

[1] Mel'-le-a-loo'-mah is the name of the hill-country south of Lower Lake--between Lower Lake and Coyote Valley.

blue oak tree, the kind called moo-le. [1] When the geese, which were walking on the ground, came up to this tree, Wek'-wek took careful aim with his low'-ke and let fly and the stone flew down among them and killed more than two hundred, and then came back to his hand. He at once fired again and killed several hundred more. He then gathered them all and packed them on his head back to Tu'-le-yo'-me and gave them to his grandfather, Ol'-le the Coyote-man.

Next morning when Wek'-wek was sitting on top of the roundhouse he saw someone coming. It was Sah'-te the Weasel-man, who lives under the ground; he passed on to the south without stopping. Wek'-wek said, "This looks like a man. Who is this man? Tomorrow morning I'll go and see." So next morning he went out again and sat on top of the roundhouse. Soon he saw Sah'-te coming; he came from the north and went off to the south. Then Wek'-wek also went south; he went to the sharp peak, Loo-peek'-pow'-we, and saw Sah'-te pass and go still farther south.

Ol'-le the Coyote-man and Wek'-wek the Falcon-man at their Roundhouse

---

[1] My informant pointed out this little old tree to me and said that when he was a little boy his father told him that it had always been there, just as it was in the days of Wek'-wek.

Wek'-wek returned to Tu'-le-yo'-me and presently saw Sah'-te come and go north again toward Clear Lake. Wek'-wek wanted to find out where Sah'-te lived, so he went up to Clear Lake and at the head of Sulphurbank Bay he found Sah'-te's lah'-mah (roundhouse). He said to himself, "Now I've got you," and went into Sah'-te's house. But Sah'-te was not at home. Wek'-wek looked around and saw a great quantity of hoo'-yah, the shell beads or money. It was in skin sacks. He took these sacks--ten or twelve of them-- and emptied the shell money out on a bear skin robe and packed it on his head back to Tu'-le-yo'-me. But he did not take it in to show his grandfather; he hid it in a small creek near by and did not say anything about it.

When Sah'-te came home he found that his beads were gone. "Who stole my beads?" he asked.

He then took his yah'-tse [the stick the people used to wear crossways in a twist of their back hair] and stood it up in the fire, and oo'-loop the flame climbed it and stood on the top. He then took the yah'-tse with the flame at one end and said he would find out who stole his shell money. First he pointed it to the north, but nothing happened; then to the west, and nothing happened; then east; then up; then down, and still nothing happened. Then he pointed it south toward Tu'-le-yo'-me and the flame leaped from the stick and spread swiftly down the east side of Lower Lake, burning the grass and brush and making a great smoke.

In the evening Wek'-wek came out of the roundhouse at Tu'-le-yo'-me and saw the country to the north on fire. He went in and told his grandfather that something was burning on Clear Lake.

Ol'-le the Coyote-man answered, "That's nothing; the people up there are burning tules."

Ol'-le knew what Wek'-wek had done, and knew that Sah'-te had sent the fire, for Ol'-le was a magician and knew everything, but he did not tell Wek'-wek that he knew.

After a while Wek'-wek came out again and looked at the fire and saw that it was much nearer and was coming on swiftly. He was afraid, and went back and told his grandfather that the fire was too near and too hot and would soon reach them. After a little he went out again and came back and said, "Grandfather, the fire is coming fast; it is on this side of the lake and is awfully hot."

Ol'-le answered, "That's nothing; the people at Lower Lake are burning tules." But now the roar and heat of the fire were terrible, even inside the roundhouse, and Wek'-wek thought they would soon burn. He was so badly frightened that he told his grandfather what he had done. He said, "Grandfather, I stole Sah'-te's hoo'-yah and put it in the creek, and now I'm afraid we shall burn."

Then Ol'-le took a sack and came out of the roundhouse and struck the sack against an oak tree, and fog came out. He struck the tree several times and each time more fog came out and spread around.

Then he went back in the house and got another sack and beat the tree, and more fog came, and then rain. He said to Wek'-wek, "It is going to rain for ten days and ten nights." And it did rain, and the rain covered the whole country till all the land and all the hills and all the mountains were under water--everything except the top of Oo-de'-pow-we (Mount Konokti, on the west side of Clear Lake) which was so high that its top stuck out a little.

There was no place for Wek'-wek to go and he flew about in the rain till he was all tired out. Finally he found the top of Oo-de'-pow-we and sat down on it and stayed there.

On the tenth day the rain stopped, and after that the water began to go down and each day the mountain stood up higher. Wek'-wek stayed on the mountain about a week, by which time the water had gone down and the land was bare again. In Clear Lake near Oo-de'-pow-we is an island which was the home of two small grebes, diving birds, called Hoo-poos'-min. They were brothers and had a roundhouse, and in the roundhouse a fire. Wek'-wek went there and stayed two or three days, and then said he was going back to Tu'-le-yo'-me.

"All right," answered the Hoo-poos'-min brothers, "but don't tell Ol'-le that we have fire."

"All right," answered Wek'-wek, and he went off to Tu'-le-yo'-me to see Ol'-le, his grandfather.

When Wek'-wek arrived Ol'-le asked: "Who are you? I'm Ol'-le, and I live at Tu'-le-yo'-me."

Wek'-wek answered, "I'm Wek'-wek and I also live at Tu'-le-yo'-me."

"Oh yes," said Ol'-le, "you are Hoi'-poo (Captain) Wek'-wek."

"Yes," answered Wek'-wek.

At that time there were no real people in the world and Wek'-wek said, "There are no people; I'm lonesome; what are we going to do?"

Then Ol'-le told Wek'-wek to bring the feathers of the geese he had killed at Wen'-nok Lake. Wek'-wek did so, and they set out and traveled over the country. Wherever they found a good place for people Ol'-le took two feathers and laid them down side by side on the ground--two together side by side in one place, two together side by side in another place, and so on in each place where he wanted a rancheria; and at the same time he gave each place its name.

Wek'-wek on the hilltop killing Geese with his Sling

Next morning they again went out and found that all the feathers had turned into people; that each pair of feathers had become two people, a man and a woman, so that at each place there were a man and a woman. This is the way all the rancherias were started.

By and by all the people had children and after a while the people became very numerous.

Wek'-wek was pleased and said, "This is good." A little later he asked, "Grandfather, now that we have people, what are we going to do? There is no fire; what can we do to get fire?"

Ol'-le replied, "I don't know; we shall see pretty soon."

Ol'-le had a small box in his roundhouse and in it kept two little Shrew-mice of the kind called We'-ke-wil'-lah. They were brothers. Ol'-le said to them: "Kah'-kah-te the Crow has fire in his roundhouse, far away in the east; you go and steal it."

We'-ke-wil'-lah the little Shrew-mice said they would try, and set out on their long journey and went far away to the east and finally came to Kah'-kah-te's roundhouse. They heard Kah'-kah-te say, "kah'-ahk," and saw a spark of fire come out of the hole on top of the house. Then they went to a dead tree and got some too-koom' (the kind of buckskin that comes on dead wood) and cut off a piece and took it and climbed up on top of Kah'-kah-te's house and sat by the smoke hole and waited. After a while Kah'-kah-te again said "kah'-ahk," and another spark came out, but they could not reach it. But the next time Kah'-kah-te said "kah'-ahk" and another spark came out the little brothers caught it in their too-koom', the wood buckskin.

When they had done this they caught a little bug and pushed him in backward till he touched the spark. Then they said, "Let's go," and set out at once and traveled as fast as they could toward Tu'-le-yo'-me.

Just then Kah'-kah-te the Crow came out of his house and in the darkness saw a little speck of light moving back and forth among the trees. It was the fire bug going home with the little Shrew brothers. Kah'-kah-te when he saw it cried, "Somebody has stolen my fire," and set out in pursuit.

The little brothers and the firefly were badly frightened and ran around a little hill so Kah'-kah-te could not see them, and hid under the bank of a dry creek. Kah'-kah-te hunted for them for some time but could not find them and went back to his house. His mate, who was inside, said, "Nobody stole our fire."

Kah'-kah-tę answered, "Yes, someone stole it, I saw it go around." Then he went back into his house.

Then the We'-ke-wil'-lah brothers ran as fast as they could all the way back to Tu'-le-yo'-me and arrived there the same night. They said to Ol'-le, "Grandfather, look," and tossed him the too-koom'--the tree buckskin with the fire inside. He unrolled it and found the fire and took it out and made a fire on the ground.

Wek'-wek exclaimed, "That is good; I'm glad; now everybody can have fire."

Then Ol'-le put the fire in the oo'-noo (buckeye) tree, and told the people how to rub the oo'-noo stick to make it come out. From that time to this everybody has known how to get fire from the oo'-noo tree.

HOW CHA'-KA THE TULE-WREN SHOT OUT THE SUN

CHA'-KA the Tule-wren was a poor worthless boy. He had no father and no mother and went from house to house begging, and the people gave him food to eat. Nobody liked him, and finally they tired of feeding him. One day he told them that if they did not give him food he would shoot out the Sun. Then everybody laughed. Again he said he surely would shoot it out. They said, "Go ahead and shoot."

So he did; he sent his arrow right up into the Sun and let the light out and the whole world became dark. There was no Sun, no Moon, no Stars, no Fire-everything was dark. It was dark for years and years and the people could not see to find food, and everybody was starving.

All this time O'-ye the Coyote-man was thinking how he could get the Sun and light back again. At length he saw just a little light a long way off. He sent Koo-loo'-pe the Humming-bird to steal it.

Koo-loo'-pe set out on the long journey and finally came to the fire and stole a little piece and brought it back under his chin--you can see the blaze there to this day.

When he was bringing it somebody chased him, but he was so small and flew so swiftly they could not see which way he went and could not catch him. So he escaped with the fire and brought it back to O'-ye the Coyote-man, and the people had light again.

HOW WEK'-WEK WAS SAVED FROM THE FLOOD

O'-YE the Coyote-man, and Wek'-wek the Falcon-man quarrelled. Then O'-ye gathered up the people and took them away with him across the ocean, leaving Wek'-wek alone. Then he made the rain come and cover the world with water. The water grew deeper and deeper and covered all the trees and all the hills and all the mountains until nothing was left but water.

Wek'-wek could find no place to rest--nothing to stand on--and had to fly and fly and fly till he was all tired out. By and by he could fly no longer and fell on the water and was floating around nearly dead when his wing caught on a little stick. This stick stuck up from the top of the roundhouse of Pe'-leet the Grebe, who came up to see what was the matter. He found Wek'-wek (a relative of his) nearly drowned and pulled him down into his roundhouse and saved him.

Then O'-ye the Coyote-man let the water down and brought the people back.

WHY THE BODEGA BAY INDIANS CAN NOT STAND COLD

WHEN O'-ye the Coyote-man had everything ready he thought he would make people. So he gathered a lot of sticks of different kinds--some hard, as oak, madrone, and manzanita; some soft and hollow, as the sage-herb--and made a big pile of them and said that by and by they would turn into people.

Then he went over all the country and whereever he wanted a village he laid down two sticks, and gave the place a name--and the name he gave it then has always been its name and is its name to this day. Then he went away.

In a short time the sticks turned into people, and all the rancherias were started with the first real people.

In places where he had put sticks of hard wood the people were strong and well and warm-blooded and could stand cold weather; but in places where he put poor wood the people were weak and sickly and could not stand cold weather. Here at Bodega Bay he left only sticks of Po'-to-po'-to the sage-herb, [1] which has a hollow stem and has no strength. That is the reason our people are tender and weak and can not stand cold, and why nearly all died soon after the white men came. We are hollow inside and can not stand cold.

---

[1] The sage-herb is a form of Artemisia ludoviciana.

YEL'-LO-KIN AND OO-WEL'-LIN, THE MAN-EATING GIANTS

WE'-PI-AHK the Eagle was chief of the First People. He took for his wife Tu'-pe the Kangaroo-rat. She did not stay at home nights because night was the time she went out to hunt for food. We'-pi-ahk did not understand this and when she came back one morning he beat her and killed her. After that he stayed at home a month and cried and never went out. When the month was up he stopped crying and went out in the sun.

Next day Yel'-lo-kin came. Yel'-lo-kin was a giant bird--the biggest bird in the world. He was in the habit of carrying off children--boys and girls up to fourteen or fifteen years of age. He took them by the top of the head and carried them up through the hole in the middle of the sky to his home on top of the sky, where he killed and ate them.

Yel'-lo-kin had a wife. She was Ol'-lus muk-ki'-e the Toad-woman, the aunt of We'-pi-ahk the Eagle. Yel'-lo-kin had stolen her from the earth and had taken her up to his house above the sky. He did not kill her but kept her as his wife, and brought people to her to eat; but she would not eat people.

When We'-pi-ahk the Eagle had gone out in the sun Yel'-lo-kin came and caught him by the top of his head and carried him up through the hole in the sky.

A boy playing outside saw this and shouted to the people, and they all got poles and bows and arrows and tried to reach Yel'-lo kin but could not, and Yel'-lo-kin went on up with We'-pi-ahk and took him to his house on top of the sky and left him there. When We'-pi-ahk looked around he saw his aunt, Ol'-lus muk-ki'-e the Toad-woman. She told him to look out, that in a little while Yel'-lo-kin would come back and kill him. "He will take you to a big tank of blood and ask if you want to drink," she said. "When he does this you must answer 'yes' and pretend to reach down, and tell him the water is too low, you can't reach it; you are afraid of falling in. Ask him to show you how to get it."

"All right," answered We'-pi-ahk--he would do as she said.

Then she gave him a big stone knife with which to cut off Yel'-lo-kin's head.

Soon Yel'-lo-kin returned and did exactly as his wife said he would do. When he asked We'-pi-ahk to drink, We'-pi-ahk told him he could not reach the water; he was afraid of falling in, and asked Yel'-lo-kin to show him how. Then Yel'-lo-kin leaned over and reached down deep in the tank, and We'-pi-ahk struck him with the big knife and cut off his head, whereupon Yel'-lo-kin banged around inside the tank and flapped his big wings and made a great noise, and finally flopped out and died outside. He stretched out his wings and they were as big as pine trees. Then We'-pi-ahk was free.

Ah-hā'-le the Coyote-man was down below. We'-pi-ahk the Eagle was his uncle. Ah-hā'-le asked the people, "Where is my uncle, We'-pi-ahk?"

The boys told him he had gone up--that Yel'-lo-kin had carried him up through the sky. Ah-hā'-le looked but could not see the hole they had gone through. Then he went south and looked for the south hole in the sky, but could not find it. Returning, he went north to the hole at Thunder Mountain, but could not get in that way for it was too cold. Then he came back to the village and sprang up high in the air and passed through the middle hole in the sky-the same hole that Yel'-lo-kin had gone through with We'-pi-ahk.

Just as he arrived, at that very moment We'-pi-ahk struck Yel'-lo-kin with the knife and killed him, and Ah-hā'-le saw him die.

"It is a good thing that you killed him," Ah-hā'-le said.

We'-pi-ahk replied, "He has been stealing our boys and girls; whenever he was hungry he went down and got a boy or a girl. We lost lots of people."

Then We'-pi-ahk showed Ah-hā'-le the tank of blood where Yel'-lo-kin had done his killing.

After a while Ah-hā'-le asked, "What are you going to do with Yel'-lo-kin?"

We'-pi-ahk said he was going to burn him, so he would not come to life again.

But Ah-hā'-le replied, "No uncle, you had better not burn him."

Then We'-pi-ahk asked, "What are you going to do with him?"

Ah-ha'-le answered, "I think I'll cut off his wings and take them down home."

"What are you going to do with them?" asked We'-pi-ahk.

Ah-hā'-le replied, "I'm going to plant the big feathers and make trees. If I plant plenty of trees and everything green, there will be many people, for when I'm done planting trees I'm going to make people."

When he had finished speaking he went down to the earth through a hole of his own, for he was a witch doctor.

After he had gone down, Yel'-lo-kin's wife, Ol'-lus muk-ki'-e the Toad-woman, asked We'-pi-ahk how he was going to get down.

"I don't know," answered We'-pi-ahk.

"I'll take you down," said Ol'-lus muk-ki'-e.

"How," asked We'-pi-ahk.

"You will see how," she replied. And she gathered the strong green sword-grass called kis'-soo, that grows by the river, and made a long rope of it and with it let We'-pi-ahk down to the earth.

Ah-hā'-le the Coyote-man planted the feathers, and when they had come up watched them grow. They grew into grasses, wild oats, flowers, manzanitas, and other bushes, and into yellow pines, sugar pines, black oaks, blue oaks, and other kinds of trees. He told them all to bear seed every year so the people who were coming would have plenty to eat. He also made rivers and rocks--Yel'-lo-kin's heart he turned into a black rock.

When he had done this he made people. These also he made by planting feathers. The people multiplied and in a short time their villages were everywhere in the land.

O-WEL'-LIN THE ROCK GIANT

THERE was a great Giant who lived in the north. His name was Oo-wel'-lin, and he was as big as a pine tree. When he saw the country full of people he said they looked good to eat, and came and carried them off and ate them. He could catch ten men at a time and hold them between his fingers, and put more in a net on his back, and carry them off. He would visit a village and after eating all the people would move on to another, going southward from his home in the north. When he had gone to the south end of the world and had visited all the villages and eaten nearly all the people--not quite all, for a few had escaped--he turned back toward the north. He crossed the Wah-kal'-mut-ta (Merced River) at a narrow place in the canyon about six miles above Op'-lah (Merced Falls) where his huge footprints may still be seen in the rocks) showing the exact place where he stepped from Ang-e'-sa-wā'-pah on the south side to Hik-kā'-nah on the north side. When night came he went into a cave in the side of a round-topped hill over the ridge from Se-saw-che [a little south of the present town of Coulterville].

The people who had escaped found his sleeping place in the cave and shot their arrows at him but were not able to hurt him, for he was a rock giant.

When he awoke he was hungry and took the trail to go hunting. Then the people said to Oo'-choom the Fly: "Go follow Oo-wel'-lin and when he is hot bite him all over, on his head, on his eyes and ears, and all over his body, everywhere, all the way down to the bottoms of his feet, and find out where he can be hurt.

"All right," answered Oo'-choom the Fly, and he did as he was told. He followed Oo-wel'-lin and bit him everywhere from the top of his head, all the way down to his feet without hurting him, till finally he bit him under the heel. This made Oo-wel'-lin kick. Oo'-choom waited, and when the giant had fallen asleep bit him under the heel of the other foot, and he kicked again. Then Oo'-choom told the people.

When the people heard this they took sharp sticks and long sharp splinters of stone and set them up firmly in the trail, and hid nearby and watched.

After a while Oo-wel'-lin came back and stepped on the sharp points till the bottoms of his feet were stuck full of them. This hurt him dreadfully, and he fell down and died.

When he was dead the people asked, "Now he is dead, what are we to do with him?"

And they all answered that they did not know.

But a wise man said, "We will pack wood and make a big fire and burn him."

Then everyone said, "All right, let's burn him," and they brought a great quantity of dry wood and made a big fire and burned Oo-wel'-lin the Giant. When he began to burn, the wise man told everybody to watch closely all the time to see if any part should fly off to live again, and particularly to watch the whites of his eyes. So all the people watched closely all the time he was burning. His flesh did not fly off; his feet did not fly off; his hands did not fly off; but by and by the whites of his eyes flew off quickly--so quickly indeed that no one but Chik'-chik saw them go. Chik'-chik was a small bird whose eyes looked sore, but his sight was keen and quick. He was watching from a branch about twenty feet above the Giant's head and saw the whites of the eyes fly out. He saw them fly out and saw where they went and quickly darted after them and brought them back and put them in the fire again, and put on more wood and burnt them until they were completely consumed.

The people now made a hole and put Oo-wel'lin's ashes in it and piled rocks on the place and watched for two or three days. But Oo-wel'-lin was dead and never came out.

Then the wise man asked each person what he would like to be, and called their names. Each answered what animal he would be, and forthwith turned into that animal and has remained the same to this day.

This was the beginning of the animals as they are now-the deer, the ground squirrel, the bear, and other furry animals; the bluejay, the quail, and other birds of all kinds, and snakes and frogs and the yellowjacket wasp and so on.

Before that they were Hoi-ah'-ko--the FIRST PEOPLE.

TIM-ME-LA'-LE THE THUNDER

WHEN Oo-wel'-lin the Giant was traveling south over the country eating people, there were two little boys, brothers, who were out hunting when he was at their village, and, so escaped. When they came home they found that their father and mother and all the other people had been killed and eaten.

The younger one asked the other, "What shall we do? Shall we live here, only two of us? Maybe you are clever enough to turn into some other kind of thing and never die."

The elder brother did not know; he was stupid; the younger was the bright one.

For about a month they hunted birds and ate them; they had no acorn mush or other food, nothing but birds. One day they made a little hut of brush (called o-hoo'-pe) by a spring where the birds came to drink. Here they killed a great many birds of different kinds.

The younger brother said, "Let us save all the feathers of the birds we kill-wing feathers and tail feathers and all."

Soon they had enough for both, and the younger said, "We have enough. Let's be big birds and never die--never grow old."

"How are we to do it?" asked the elder brother.

The younger answered, "You know how the big birds spread their wings and go, without bothering to eat or drink."

In a few days they took the big wing-feathers they had saved and stuck them in a row along their arms, and soon had wings; and then they stuck other feathers all over their bodies and soon were covered with feathers, like big birds.

Then the younger brother said: "You fly; let me see you fly a little way." The elder brother tried but could not make his wings go.

"Try again and I'll help," said the younger, and he pushed his brother along; but though he tried again he could not fly, and dropped down.

Then they took more feathers and set them closer so they would not leak air. When they had done this the younger asked: "Do you think you can go this time?"

But the elder one replied, "Let's see you try."

"All right," the younger answered, and flew a little way.

"Now you try," he called, and lifted his brother up and pushed him to help him start, but when he had flown a little way he cried out that he could not go any farther.

"Go on, I'm coming," called the younger, and he soon caught up and came under his brother and sailed round and round and went up into the air and came down.

The Orphan Boys killing Ducks and Geese by the River. "For a month they hunted birds and ate them"

Then the younger said, "Now we can fly, what kind of animal shall we be?"

The elder answered that he did not know.

The younger said, "How about We-ho'-whe-mah, who lives on the water in the back country?"

"All right," replied the other. So they flew again, and the younger helped start the elder and flew under him so as to catch him if he fell, and they flew up and down and around.

The younger again asked his brother if he would like to be We-ho'-whe-mah.

The brother replied, "No, I don't want to live on the water."

"Then how would you like to be Tim-me-lā'-le the Thunder," asked the younger. "We could come back sometimes and make a big noise and frighten the people. In summer we could go up through the north hole in the sky and stay up above the sky, and in winter come back here and make a big noise and rain to make the country green. Then maybe the people would come back and live again. We once had a father and mother and sister and uncle and grandfather and others. Maybe they would come back. We want to help them; we could make good rain to make things grow-- acorns, pine nuts, grass, and all. Then maybe the people would come back and eat. We should never use food, never drink water, never grow old, and never be killed."

"All right," answered the elder, "We shall live always. But how are we going to make rain?"

"I'll show you," answered the younger. And they started again and went up very slowly, way up to the sky, and went north and found the north hole and went through it. When near the sky, but before they had gone through, the younger began to make a loud rumbling noise; it was Tim-me-lā'-le the Thunder. [1] The elder tried but failed. The younger told him to try again. He did so and in a short time made thunder all right. Then they went through the hole and up above the sky into the Yel'-lo-kin country.

---

[1] Tim-me-lā'-le is rolling thunder; the sharp crash is Kah'-loo.

When winter time came the younger said, "Come, let us go back." So they came down through the hole in the sky and traveled south and saw that people were there already. Then they shouted and made thunder and rain. After that they returned home through the north hole in the sky. And every winter even to this day they come back and thunder and make rain to make things grow for the people.

WEK'-WEK'S SEARCH FOR HIS FATHER

AH-HA'-LE the Coyote-man told the people that there were four holes in the sky--one in the north, one in the south, one in the east, and one in the west. In those days Tim-me-lā'-le the Thunder came outof the north hole in winter and went back about May, just as he does now.

At this time Wek'-wek the Falcon was not yet born. His father, Yi-'yil, had gone far away to the south, where he had been killed before Wek'-wek's birth.

When Wek'-wek was fourteen years old he already had two or three wives, one of whom was Yow'-hah the Mallard Duck. He asked her if she was old enough to have seen his father. She replied, "No."

He then traveled all about and asked all the people who his father was and where he had gone, but no one could tell him. Then he went out to search; he traveled north, south, east, and west, but could find no trace of his father and no one could tell him where he had gone.

Then Wek'-wek transformed himself into a witch doctor and said, "Now I know where my father went, I smell him."

At sundown he came home to Yow'-hah his wife, and when she had fallen asleep he took a forked limb of a tree and put it in the bed beside her. Then he went down into a hole in the ground and came up near the village [thus leaving no tracks]. Then he went south.

In the morning Yow'-hah awoke and found the forked limb and pushed it away saying, "What's the matter with my husband?" She asked his other wives if they had seen which way he went--"Which way did our husband go?" she asked.

They replied, "Go away, you live with him, we don't."

Then Yow'-hah went away and cried. She cried for a day or so, but no one could tell her which way Wek'-wek had gone.

She then took a crooked acorn stick and stuck it in the ground and the stick sprang south. Then she knew the way he had gone, and quickly prepared some baskets of food and set out to follow him.

After a while she overtook him, bringing him the food. By this time Wek'-wek was very tired and had fallen down on the side of the trail. He had a partner, Hoo-loo'-e the Dove, who accompanied him. He said to Hoo-loo'-e, "The old woman is coming behind; I am going to shoot her." But when she came he could not pull the arrow. She went to him and said, "You are hungry; I've brought you food."

He was angry and would not answer. He said to Hoo-loo'-e his partner, "You are hungry, you had better eat."

Hoo-loo'-e replied, "Yes, I think I am hungry."

"Well, eat," said Wek'-wek, and Hoo-loo'-e ate.

Wek'-wek was angry and would not eat. He told his wife to go home and not follow him. He said: "I go to a bad place; I follow my father; nobody can get through the hole in the sky; you go home."

She answered, "No, I'll not go home, I'll follow you."

Then Wek'-wek continued on the trail of his father.

Wek'-wek had an aunt, Ol'-lus muk-ki'-e the Toad-woman. Her husband was O-wah'-to, the big-headed Fire Lizard. He had a fire which he could send to burn people.

Wek'-wek told Hoo-loo'-e his partner to go around another way with Yow'-hah his wife while he stopped to talk to his aunt's husband, O-wah'-to. Again he told his wife to go home, but she would not. Then Wek'-wek went to the place where O-wah'-to lived. He saw his aunt Ol'-lus muk-ki'-e outside, cracking acorns, and went to her to get something to eat.

O-wah'-to, who was inside the house, called out "Who's there?" and his wife answered, "Nobody." Then he heard Wek'-wek take another step, and called out again, "Who's there?" and again his wife answered, "Nobody, only Oo'-choom the Fly." She whispered to Wek'-wek to step very softly and to eat very quickly--to hurry and eat and go.

But O-wah'-to heard him and exclaimed, "Somebody is out there sure," and he came out and saw Wek'-wek, and sent his fire to burn him.

Wek'-wek ran and ran as fast as he could and caught up with Hoo-loo'-e and Yow'-hah, but the fire chased them and burnt so quickly and came so fast that they had not time to reach the hole in the sky. So they turned and ran down to the low country and climbed up on a high rock; but the fire kept on and burned the rock. Then they rushed to the ocean, but the fire dashed after them and made the water boil. Then they hastened north to another big rock, as high as a hill, and climbed on top; but the fire pursued and burnt that rock also. Then they climbed up into the sky, but the fire pressed on and came so close that it singed the tail of Wek'-wek's quiver. Then they ran down into the low country again and found a crack in the ground and all three crawled into it. But the fire came and burnt down into the crack and drove them out.

By this time Wek'-wek's wife, Yow'-hah, had become very tired from so much running, and gave out. She said to her husband, "You are of no account. Why don't you put out that fire? I would like to see you make a pond half a mile wide."

"I'll try," he answered and shot an arrow of the kow'-woo wood (the buttonball bush) into the ground and water came up through the hole and continued to rise until they all stood in water, but still the fire beset them and made the water boil. Yow'-hah said she thought she would die. Then Wek'-wek shot an arrow into the ground in another place and a spring of water came and green stuff grew around the edges; but the fire continued and made the water boil as before.

Again Yow'-hah said, "You are of no account; you would die if I had not followed you."

Wek'-wek answered, "All right, you try."

Yow'-hah took a tule and threw it, and a big spring burst out, bordered all around with a broad belt of green tules; and they stepped into the spring and the fire could not reach them-it could not burn the green tules. So the fire went out and there was no more fire. Yow'-hah the old woman had stopped the fire. She was proud of this and said, "You see, if I had stayed at home you would be dead; if I go you will be all right." And the three continued on together.

By and by they came to the hole--the south hole in the sky. Then Wek'-wek said, "You two had better go home, you can't get through the hole."

His wife answered "No," and tried to go through but failed.

Wek'-wek shot an arrow through, but the hole closed so quickly that it caught the arrow and broke it. He again said to the others, "You can't get through." Then he tried and jumped so quickly that he went through. Then Hoo-loo'-e his partner tried, and likewise jumped very quickly and got through, and the sky did not catch him. Then Yow'-hah had to try again. Wek'-wek told her she must go through or go back. But she was too big and too slow. She said, "You will have to take me through." So he went back and got her and put her into his dog-skin quiver and jumped through with her. As they passed through, the hole closed and caught her feet and crushed them flat-that is why all ducks have flat feet.

Now all three were through.

In the south, beyond the hole in the sky, were other people. They had two chiefs, Ho'-ho the Turkey Buzzard, and Koo'-choo a huge shaggy beast of great strength and fierceness. Tap-pitch'-koo-doot the Kingbird lived there, and Hok'-ke-hok'-ke also.

Before Wek'-wek arrived, Captain Ho'-ho the Buzzard said to the people, "I dreamed that a north Indian is coming--the son of Yi'-yil, the man we burned. Everybody watch; maybe we shall have a good time again." So everybody watched.

After a while the watchers saw Wek'-wek coming. They saw him come through the hole. Then they ran back and told the people. This made the people happy, and they made ready to play the ball game.

When Wek'-wek reached the village he saw his father's widow there crying, with her hair cut short in mourning. He asked her, "Did my father die here?"

"Yes," she answered, and added, "Your father had plenty of money when he lost the game, but the chiefs Koo'-choo and Ho'-ho would not take the money; they were playing for his life; they wanted to burn him. Old Koo'-choo made a circle around the fire and made your father stand in the middle, and told him not to die too soon. After he had been burning a little while Koo'-choo asked how far the fire had burned, and Yi'-yil answered, 'to my knees, I'm going to die.'

"'No, don't die yet,' said Koo'-choo; and he asked again, 'How far has the fire burned now?'

"Yi'-Yil answered, 'to my belly, and I'm going to die now.'

"'No, don't die yet,' said Koo'-choo, and he asked again, 'How far has the fire burned now?'

"'To my heart,' replied Yi'-yil, 'and I'm going to die now.'

"'No, no,' again said Koo'-choo, 'don't die yet; how far has the fire burned now?'

"'To my shoulders and I'm going to die,' said Yi'yil.

"'No, don't die yet; how far has the fire burned now?'

"'To my mouth, and I'm going to die,' answered Yi'-yil.

"'No, not yet, there's plenty of time yet,' said Koo'-choo; 'how far has it burned now?'

"'To my eyes, it's burning my eyes now and I'm going to die,' replied Yi'-yil.

"'No, no,' said Koo'-choo, 'don't die yet;' and when he saw that the fire had reached the top of Yi'-yil's head he asked again and for the last time, 'How far has it burned now?'

"There was no reply, and he knew, and all the people knew, that Yi'-yil was burned to death and was dead."

This is what Yi'-yil's widow, who had seen the burning, told Wek'-wek.

Wek'-wek was very angry; he knew that the people wanted to burn him as they had burned Yi'-yil his father; and he made up his mind what he would do. He left his wife Yow'-hah with Koo'-choo and the others and told her to entertain them. He then, asked his father's widow which way they had taken his father to play the ball game. She told him, and he followed his father's trail. He found gopher holes in the trail, and holes the people had made for the ball to fall into so he would lose the game, and he filled them up. He came back over Koo'-choo's trail by daylight and found it all right-all the holes filled up and no holes left.

When he returned he found that the two firemen, Lol'-luk the Woodrat and No-put'-kul-lol the Screech Owl, had the fire all ready to burn him, but he said nothing.

Early next morning they all set out down the trail to play the ball game. Wek'-wek played so fast that old Koo'-choo became very tired and nearly gave out. He shot out a terrible skunk-like smell to make Wek'-wek sick, but Wek'-wek kept ahead and was not harmed.

Wek'-wek won the game and came back first; all the others were tired and Koo'-choo came in half dead.

When they had returned, Yow'-hah, Wek'-wek's wife, told Wek'-wek to burn Koo'-choo first.

Koo'-choo said to Wek'-wek: "You have won the game; everybody will bring you money; here is the money; you take it."

Wek'-wek answered, "No, I'll not take it. You would not take my father's money; you took his life."

Then they brought two more sacks full of money, but Wek'-wek pushed it away. He seized the two wicked chiefs, Koo'-choo and Ho'ho; he seized them by their arms and threw them into the fire that had been prepared for him, and took the others in the same way and threw them all in the fire.

Some ran away and tried to hide, but Wek'-wek went after them and brought them back and threw them in the fire-men, women, and children-- and burned them all. He then called the firemen to come--Lol'-luk the Woodrat and No-put'-kul-lol the Screech Owl--but they cried and refused to come. Then he took his bow and arrow and shot them and pitched them into the fire and they were burned like the rest.

The only people not burned were two witch doctors--Pel-pel'-nah the Nuthatch and Choo-ta-tok'-kwe-lah the Red-headed Sapsucker. They lived in the big ceremonial house and never came out; they never ate and never drank. Wek'-wek asked them, "Shall I come in?"

They answered "Yes."

Wek'-wek went inside and said: "You two are witch doctors; you never eat and never drink and never see people. Do you think you can make my father live again? I'll pay you. I want to see my father. I want to see what he is like."

They answered that they would try. One said to the other: "We will try; yes, we must try; but how shall we do it?" Then they took a jointed rod of la'-hah (the wild cane) and put Yi'-yil's burnt bones in the hollow inside, and put three or four feathers on the outside, like an arrow. Then Choo-ta-tok'-kwe-lah asked Wek'-wek for his bow, and took it and shot the cane arrow high up into the air; and when it was way up, Yi'-yil came slowly out of the hole in the end and sailed around and around, coming lower and lower, till he came down where the others were.

Then Wek'-wek asked him, "Are you my father? You don't look as I supposed."

Yi'-yil answered, "Yes, I'm Yi'-yil your father."

Wek'-wek said, "I've burned all the people here. Will you go home with me? Are you sure you are my father?"

"Yes," answered Yi'-yil, "I'm your father and I'll go home with you."

"All right," said Wek'-wek, "Let's go."

After a while, when they had gone a little way, Wek'-wek turned and said, "I think you had better not go with me. You look queer--only half like us. You go to the other side of the mountain down on the coast" (meaning Oo'-yum-bel'-le, Mount Diablo). Then Yi'-yil went back into the cane arrow, and Wek'-wek, his wife Yow'-hah, and his partner Hoo-loo'-e returned through the hole in the sky that they had gone through on their way south.

When they were on the other side, Wek'-wek said to his wife: "Old woman, you may have to run again. I'm going to kill O-wah'-to, my uncle-in-law, who chased us with fire and tried to destroy us when we were here before." So he sent Yow'-hah and Hoo-loo'-e ahead and told them to wait for him while he proceeded to O-wah'-to's place. He went there and shot O-wah'-to with an arrow and killed him dead the first shot.

Then they continued on, and when they had gone a few miles, they came to another fireman, whose name was Hos-sok'-kil-wah. Wek'-wek sent his wife and partner ahead as before while he went alone to fight Hos-sok'-kil-wah. He took an arrow with a point of white flint stone, and shot and killed Hos-sok'-kil-wah, who at once turned into the white flint fire rock. And so they continued, Wek'wek killing all the bad people on the way.

WEK-WEK'S SEARCH FOR HIS SISTER

AFTER Wek'-wek, Hoo-loo'-e and Yow'-hah had returned home, Wek'-wek said, "I have heard that I once had a sister; where is my sister?"

No one answered.

Then Wek'-wek slept and dreamed. Then he went off alone to the north and told no one.

Wek'-wek had a nephew, Ah'-ut the Crow. Ah'-ut asked the people, "Where is my uncle?" No one answered. Then Ah'-ut said he would find him, and he also set out for the north. Finding that he could not catch up with Wek'-wek he shot an arrow and the arrow went over Wek'-wek's head and fell just beyond.

Wek'-wek knew who had shot it, and said, "Who told my nephew?"

When Ah'-ut came up, Wek'-wek asked, "Why do you follow me? I'm searching for my sister; you go home."

"No," answered Ah'-ut, "I'll go with you."

Then Wek'-wek's brothers, two little hawks, who also had been following, overtook Wek'-wek and Ah'-ut and all went on together.

After a while they found the rancheria. It was in a big cave about two miles below Koo-loo'-te [now the town of Sonora in Tuolumne County]. Wek'-wek sent one of his little brothers into the cave. He went in and on one side of the entrance saw O-hum'-mah-te the Grizzly Bear, and on the other side He-le'-jah the Mountain Lion) but saw nothing of the sister.

Then Wek'-wek sent in the other brother. When he returned he said some one was inside cooking acorns; he had seen a woman cook the acorn soup by putting into the basket hot quail eggs instead of hot stones. He said also that farther back in the cave was something that looked like a sharp rock.

Then Ah'-ut the Crow said he would go in. When he found the woman cooking with the quail eggs he picked them up and took off the shells and ate all the eggs. Then he asked the woman, "Is my uncle's sister here?"

"Yes," she answered, "but you can't go in."

But he did go in, and when he came to He-le'-jah the Mountain Lion, he said, "You are good to eat," and shot him with an arrow and killed him. Then he turned to O-hum'mah-te the Grizzly Bear and said the same to him, and killed him also and pulled him out. Then he went in farther and saw the Sharp Rock and shot it also and killed it, and picked up his arrow and put it back in his quiver. Then he went still farther in and found Wek'-wek's sister. She was old and naked and shriveled--nothing but bare bones--for no one had given her anything to eat.

Ah'-ut returned and told Wek'-wek he could now go in, and Wek'-wek went in. When he saw his sister without clothes and all bones he felt badly and cried. Then he took her out and helped her walk, and cooked some acorns and fed her. Then he sent her home with his brothers.

WEK'-WEK'S VISIT TO THE UNDERWORLD PEOPLE

AFTER Wek'-wek had sent his sister home he stayed near the caves below Koo-loo'-te and dug holes in the sand and found roots and seeds that were good to eat. In digging he came to a very deep hole which led down under the world; he went down this hole and when he reached the underworld found other people there, and got a wife with a little boy. Besides his wife there were To-to'-kon the Sandhill Crane, Wah'-ah the Heron, Cha-poo'-kah-lah the Blackbird, and others.

To-to'-kon the Sandhill Crane was chief. When he saw Wek'-wek he said, "What shall we do with this man; he is lost; we had better kill him."

Wek'-wek saw a man make ready with his bow and arrow, and invited him to come and eat. The man came and ate, and when his belly was full went back.

Captain To-to'-kon said, "I didn't send you to eat, but to kill him." Then he sent another, and Wek'-wek asked him also to come and eat, and he did as the other had done. Then Captain To-to'-kon sent two men together to kill him, but Wek'wek called them both to come and eat) and they did so. Then To-to'-kon was angry; he sent no more men but went himself and took his bow and arrow.

Wek'-wek said to him, "Come in," whereupon To-to'-kon shot his arrow but missed.

Then Wek' wek came out and faced the people. They fired all their arrows but could not kill him. Wek'-wek said, "You can't kill me with arrows. Have you a pot big enough to hold me?"

"Yes," they answered.

"Then set it up and put me in it," he said.

And they did as they were told and put Wek'wek in the hot pot and put the cover on. When he was burned they took out the burnt bones and buried them in the ground.

Ah'-ut the Crow missed his uncle and went to his uncle's partner, Hoo-loo'-e, who was in the hole crying, and asked where Wek'-wek was. Hoo-loo'-e pointed down the hole. Ah'-ut went down and found the rancheria of the underworld people and killed them all. He then asked Wek'-wek's wife where Wek'-wek was. She answered that the people had burned and buried him.

Wek'-wek stayed in the ground five days and then came to life; he came out and asked his wife where the people were. She told him that Ah'-ut had come and killed them all. "That is too bad," he exclaimed, "I wanted to show them what kind of man I am." Then he said she should stay there and he would take the boy and go home.

She answered, "All right."

Then he shot his arrow up through the hole and caught hold of it, and held the boy also, and the arrow carried them both up to the upper world.

TAH'-LOW THE THUNDER AND TAH'-KIP' THE LIGHTNING

KOO-LA'-IS KA'-SUM the mother Deer died, leaving two boy fawns. Their uncle, O'-ye the Coyote-man, sent them away to the east, where they still live.

Once when the country was very dry an old woman who wanted water, but could not find any, went and looked at the boy fawns, and they tore her eyes out. That made Tah'-kip' the Lightning. Then they took the dry skin of Koo'-le the Bear, and shook it. That made Tah'-low the Thunder. Then Oo'-pah the Rain came.

HE'-KOO-LĀS THE SUN-WOMAN

THE world was dark. The only light anywhere was He'-koo-lās the Sun-woman. She lived far away in the east.

The people wanted light, and O'-ye the Coyote-man sent two men to bring He'-koo-lās. They traveled along time, for they had far to go. When they came to the place where she lived she refused to go back with them. So they came back alone and told O'-ye.

Then he sent more men; this time he sent enough men to bring her whether she wanted to come or not. They made the long journey to her home and tied her with ropes and brought her back to make light for the people.

Her entire body was covered with ah'-wook--the beautiful iridescent shells of the abalone; these made her shine so brightly that she gave off light and it was hard to look at her.

HOW O'-YE THE COYOTE-MAN DISCOVERED HIS WIFE

THE world was made by O'-ye the Coyote-man. The earth was covered with water. The only thing that showed above the water was the very top of Oon'-nah-pi's [Sonoma Peak, about forty miles north of San Francisco].

In the beginning O'-ye came on a raft from the west, from across the ocean. His raft was a mat of tules and split sticks; it was long and narrow. O'-ye landed on the top of Oon'-nah-pi's and threw his raft-mat out over the water--the long way north and south, the narrow way east and west; the middle rested on the rock on top of the peak. This was the beginning of the world and the world is still long and narrow like the mat--the long way north and south, the narrow way east and west.

When O'-ye was sitting alone on top of Oon'-nah-pi's, and all the rest of the world was covered with water, he saw a feather floating toward him, blown by the wind from the west--the direction from which he himself had come. He asked the feather, "Who are you?"

The feather made no reply.

He then told the feather about his family and all his relatives. When he came to mention Wek'-wek, his grandson, the feather leaped up out of the water and said, "I am Wek'-wek, your grandson."

O'-ye the Coyote-man was glad, and they talked together.

Every day O'-ye noticed Ko-to'-lah the Frog-woman sitting near him. Every time he saw her he reached out his hand and tried to catch her, but she always jumped into the water and escaped.

After four days the water began to go down, leaving more land on top of the mountain, so that Ko-to'-lah had to make several leaps to reach the water. This gave O'-ye the advantage and he ran after her and caught her.

When he had caught her he was surprised to find that she was his own wife from over the ocean. Then he was glad.

When the water went down and the land was dry O'-ye planted the buckeye and elderberry and oak trees, and all the other kinds of trees, and also bushes and grasses, all at the same time. But there were no people and he and Wek'-wek wanted people. Then O'-ye took a quantity of feathers of different kinds, and packed them up to the top of Oon'-nah-pi's and threw them up into the air and the wind carried them off and scattered them over all the country and they turned into people, and the next day there were people all over the land.

NOTE. The above story was told me at Tomales Bay by an aged Hookooeko woman, now dead, who in her early life lived at Nicasio. Another old woman, who originally came from San Rafael, gave me a slightly different version. She said that O'-ye the Coyote-man made the feathers up into four bundles, which he set in the ground in four different places--one in the west, at San Rafael; one in the east, at Sonoma; one in the north, near Santa Rosa, and one in the south, on the south side of San Francisco Bay. Next morning all had turned into people, each bundle becoming a distinct tribe, speaking a language wholly different from the languages of the others.

PART 2: PRESENT DAY MYTHS

PRESENT DAY MYTHS

IN addition to the Ancient Myths or FIRST PEOPLE stories, which relate to the early history of the world, the Mewan tribes have numerous beliefs concerning the present and the very recent past. Some of these--mainly fragments or outlines, but covering a wide range of subjects--have been collected from nearly all the extant tribes and are here brought together. They are arranged under the following headings: Beliefs concerning Animals; Beliefs concerning Ghosts and the Sign of Death; Beliefs concerning Natural Phenomena; Beliefs concerning Witches, Pigmies, Giants, and other Fabulous Beings.

BELIEFS CONCERNING ANIMALS

BEARS RESEMBLE PEOPLE AND LIKE TO DANCE

The Northern Mewuk say:

BEARS are like people. They stand up, they have hands, and when the hide is off, their bodies look like the bodies of people. Bears know a great deal. They understand the Mewuk language, and their hearing is so sharp that they hear a person a long way off and know what he says.

Bears, like people, like to dance. Once an old Indian saw some bears dance in the forest. He saw Oo-soo'-ma-te the old she Grizzly Bear and a lot of little bears. The old she Bear leaned up against a young pine tree with her left hip and bent it down, and sang moo'-oo, moo'-oo. The little bears caught hold of the bent-over tree, hanging on with their hands over their heads, while they danced with their hind feet on the ground.

HOW HE-LE'-JAH THE COUGAR HUNTS DEER

The Northern Mewuk say:

HE-le'-jah the Cougar is a hunter. He hunts O-woo'-yah the Deer. He crawls toward it like a cat, without making any noise; and when near enough makes a big leap and catches it, or knocks it downwith his long tail. When he has killed the Deer he throws his long tail around it, and packs it off on his back.

HOW TOO-LE'-ZE, THE TIMBER-WOLF HUNTS DEER

The Northern Mewuk say:

TOO-le'-ze the Big Wolf is a hunter. Like He-le'-jah the Cougar or Mountain Lion he hunts Deer, but he hunts in a different way. He chases them like Choo'-koo the Dog but catches them by the throat with his claws, which he sinks deep into the sides of the throat. In the early morning he howls long howls. He used to be common here but now is rarely seen.

TOO'-CHA-MO, THE STUMP, AND CHOO'-KOO HENG-IL'-NAH-AS'-SE, THE LOST DOG

The Northern Mewuk say:

TOO'-cha-mo the stump and Choo'-koo the dog are friends. When Choo'-koo is lost and does not know where his man has gone he goes to Too'-cha-mo and asks. Too'-cha-mo tells him which way to go to strike his man's trail; Choo'-koo goes and finds it, and no matter how far away his man is, he follows the trail right to him.

THE FIRST TEETH GO TO SOO-WAH-TAH, THE GOPHER

The Middle Mewuk of Tuolumne River say:

WHEN a child sheds its first teeth they should be saved and taken to Soo-wah-tah the Pocket Gopher, and carefully put into his hole. Then the second teeth will come quickly and grow to be strong and good.

O-LEL'-LE THE MYSTERIOUS BIRD OF THE COLD SPRINGS

The Southern Mewuk of Mariposa region say:

MANY people wear a Wep'-pah (amulet) around their necks to bring good luck and keep harm away. Some wear lucky stones, some lucky shells, some a forked feather--particularly the forked feather of a Bluejay, which is very lucky.

But the luckiest feather in the world, and the luckiest thing in the world, is a feather from O-lel'-le. O-lel'-le is a bird about the size of a Flicker, but no one ever had a good look at him. He lives in cold springs, down deep under the water, and sometimes makes the water bubble, and sometimes makes it muddy. He comes to the spring just at dark and dives down without stopping on top. In the morning just at daylight he comes up and jumps out of the water and flies away quickly, so it is very hard to see him.

Sometimes, once in a great while, a person finds one of O-lel'-le's feathers at the spring. This makes the strongest Wep'-pah in the world, and the person who finds it wears it on a string around his neck as long as he lives and always has good luck.

SOO-KOO'-ME THE GREAT HORNED OWL

The Middle Mewuk of Tuolumne River foothills say:

WHEN Soo-koo'-me the Great Horned Owl hoots, it means that someone is dying. He is himself the Ghosts of dead people. [1]

[I was once asked by a Northern Mewuk if I had ever seen the broad belt of bony plates which surrounds the eyeball of the Great Horned Owl. On replying that I had, I was assured that these closely imbricating plates are the "finger nails all jammed tight together of the ghosts caught by the owl."]

---

[1] For additional matter on this subject see Beliefs concerning Ghosts, pages 114-122. Similar beliefs are held by other California tribes.

THE MEADOWLARK, A GOSSIP AND TROUBLEMAKER

The Olayome of Putah Creek say:

HOO-yu'-mah the Meadowlark understands and speaks our language. He often makes disagreeable remarks; we often hear him say, "I see you are angry," and other mean things.

NOTE. In the Ancient Myths it has already been shown that the Northern Me'-wuk and Wi'-pā tribes of Mewan stock, and the Pā'-we-nan tribe of Midoo stock, hold the Meadowlark responsible for the failure of dead people to rise on the third or fourth day and come to life again (see pages 22-53 and 59). This belief is widespread among the Mewan tribes and is held also by at least one Pomo tribe-the `Ham'-fo or Koi'-im-fo of Clear Lake.

All the Mewan tribes, and many belonging to widely different stocks--including even the Washoo of Lake Tahoe and adjacent valleys east of the Sierra--class the Meadowlark among the bad birds. They say he talks too much and is a gossip and they do not like him. The Washoo call him Se-soo'-te'-al-le and, like several other tribes, insist that he talks to them in their own language and always makes uncomplimentary remarks. He tells them that he sees right through them; that they are stingy and provide only food enough for themselves; that they are dark on the outside only and under the skin are as white and mean as a white man, and so on.

The Mariposa Mewuk say:

If a person breaks a Meadowlark's egg it will rain.

KI'-KI'-AH THE MOUNTAIN BLUEJAY

The Middle Mewuk of Stanislaus River region say:

KI'-ki'-ah, the Crested Bluejay of the mountains, plants acorns so that oak trees come up almost everywhere.

[Several other tribes mention the same habit which, by the way, is hardly a myth.]

WHERE THE DUCKS AND GEESE GO TO BREED

The Hookooeko of Tomales Bay say:

THE home of Ducks and Geese is far up the coast in the cold country called Kon'-win, the North, which is on the other side of the sky. The way to this country lies between two high hills which continually go apart and come together, forming a sliding gateway which is ever opening and closing--the hills are never still. [1]

The name of these sliding hills is Wal-le-kah'-pah.

In spring when the Ducks and Geese go north they pass between the Wal'-le-kah'-pah hills and make their nests and rear their young in the cold Kon'-win country beyond; in fall they come back through the same opening and bring their young with them.

---

[1] The gateway in this little story is of course the North Hole in the sky, which is always described as opening and closing with great rapidity, so that only the swiftest personages can shoot through. The Wal'-le-kah'-pah hills at the north opening are evidently the same as the Thunder Mountain of other tribes, which is always close by the north hole in the sky, in the region of extreme cold.

PO'-KO-MOO THE POISON SPIDER

The Northern Mewuk say:

PO'-ko-moo the small black spider with a red spot under his belly is poison.[1] Sometimes he scratches people with his long fingers, and the scratch makes a bad sore.

The Wal'-le-kah'-pah hills at the north opening are evidently the same as the Thunder Mountain of other tribes, which is always close by the north hole in the sky, in the region of extreme cold.

[All the tribes know that this spider is poisonous and some of them make use of the poison.]

---

[1] This is true. The name of the poison spider is Lathrodectus mactens.

WHERE KOO'-TAH THE MONEY-CLAM CAME FROM

The Olamentko of Bodega Bay say:

COYOTE-man brought Koo'-tah the big clam, from which pis'-pe the shell money is made, and planted it here at Bodega Bay. [1] This is the place and the only place where the big clam was in the beginning. Wherever else you find it now, the seed came from here. The Tomales Bay people got their seed here.

---

[1] The large thick shell Bodega Bay clam from which shell money is made is Saxidomus giganteus.

BELIEFS CONCERNING GHOSTS AND THE SIGN OF DEATH

GHOSTS FOLLOW THE PATHWAY OF THE WIND

The Hookooeko of Nicasio and Tomales Bay say:

WHEN a person dies his Wal'-le [1] or Ghost goes to Hel'-wah the West, crossing the great ocean to Oo-tā-yo'-me, the Village of the Dead. In making this long journey it follows hinnan mooka, the path of the Wind. Sometimes Ghosts come back and dance in the roundhouse; sometimes people hear them dancing inside but never see them.

---

[1] In this connection it is interesting to observe that in the language of the related Olayome of Putah Creek, Bats are called Walle; while the same word in the language of the Mewan Valley tribes means Ocean. The word for ocean among the Northern Mewuk is Wallasu; among the Middle or Tuolumne Mewuk, Wallesmah.

THREE BIRDS SCREAM TO FRIGHTEN THE GHOSTS

The Southern Mewuk of the Chowchilla region say:

AFTER a person dies his Hoo'-ne or Ghost sets out toward the ocean. On the way it has to cross a broad river on a log. While it is crossing on this log, three birds scream to frighten it--Hek-ek'-ke the Quail, Ha-chah'-we the Barn Owl, and Hah'-jen-nah a small Heron.

If the Ghost is frightened and falls into the river it turns into a fish; but if it keeps on and crosses the log it continues westerly over the ocean and goes to the place where all the Ghosts live together, and never comes back.

GHOSTS MAY COME BACK IN SOO-KOO'-ME THE OWL

The Middle Mewuk of Tuolumne River say:

WHEN a person dies, Oo'leus the heart-spirit remains in the dead body for four days. During these four days everyone is quiet and the children are not allowed to run about or make a noise. On the morning of the fourth day the people sprinkle ashes on the ground over the buried basket of burnt bones--or over the grave if the corpse were buried instead of burned. On that day the heart spirit leaves the body in the invisible form of Hinnan Soos the Wind Spirit, or Soo-les'-ko the Ghost, and proceeds westward. That night it may come back in Soo-koo'-me the Owl, or in some other animal; so look out.

Some Ghosts are good, others bad. At last they all go to the ocean and cross over on a long pole to the Roundhouse of the dead, where they remain.

A HOLE IN THE NOSE SAVES TURNING INTO A FISH

The Southern Mewuk of the Mariposa region say:

IF a person dies without a hole in his nose he will turn into a fish, but if the nose is perforated for the kun-no-wah [1] he will not turn into a fish.

---

[1] The kun-no-wah is a short white rod of shell or stone worn in the nose by both men and women of this tribe.

WHAT GOOD AND BAD GHOSTS TURN INTO

The Northern Mewuk say:

THE heart-spirits or Ghosts (Soo-lek'-ko) of good Indians turn into Too-koo'-le the Great Horned Owl; those of bad Indians into Et-tā'-le the Barn Owl, Yu'-kal-loo the Meadowlark, O-lā'-choo the Coyote, or Choo'-moo-yah the Gray Fox. [1] Whatever they turn into they continue to be forever--there is no change after that.

The night after the Ghost leaves the body it may come back and do harm to someone-so it is well to look out. [My informant told me that the night after his wife's Ghost left her body it came back while he was, asleep and beat him severely.]

NOTE. The Tribes of Midoo stock also believe in transmigration. The No-to'-koi-yo or Northeastern Midoo say that their ghosts go into the Great Horned Owl, while the Pā'-we-nan or Southwestern Midoo say that when a person dies his spirit (oos) may go into any one of a number of things: it may turn into an Owl or Coyote, a Snake or a Lizard; it may become a Whirlwind, or it may go into the ground and become earth. Sometimes, but rarely, it goes off to a good place.

---

[1] The Coyote and Fox are bad--they kill too much and make too much trouble; good Indians do not like them. Yu'-kal-loo the Meadowlark is a bad bird; he is mean and is always saying disagreeable things.

GHOSTS HIDE IN STUMPS AND WHIRLWINDS

The Northern Mewuk say:

SOMETIMES when passing Too'-cha-mo the stump you hear a noise inside; it is Soo-lek'-ko the Ghost. You had better go right on, for if you stop he might do you harm.

Whenever you see Poo'-ki-yu the Whirlwind whirling the dust around and around and carrying it up into the air you may know that Soo-lek'-ko the Ghost is inside, dancing and swinging round and round. You had better not go near it but keep away.

GHOSTS HUNT FOR A BIG ANIMAL IN THE OCEAN

The Mokalumne say:

AFTER a person dies and is buried the heart-spirit comes out and shakes itself to shake off the earth, and then sails away in the air and disappears-- going northwest to the ocean. This may happen on the fourth night, or at any time between the first and fourth.

The Ghost goes to the ocean and enters the water and finds a large animal [probably a whale] whose breast it immediately lays hold of and sucks. If it does not take the breast of this animal it can not live in the ocean with the other Ghosts, but in from two to four days returns and reënters the body from which it came, and comes back to life again. It then tells the old people of the beautiful things it saw in the ocean--flowers and fishes and animals.

For a long time the people did not know where the Ul'-le or Ghosts went. After a while the Napa Indians told our people that they sometimes heard strange noises in the air overhead, usually in the evening or very early morning, sometimes at night, and more rarely in the daytime. The sounds were sometimes like singing, sometimes like crying, sometimes like calling or scolding--always high up. For a long time they did not know what these noises were, but finally some wise Indians found out that they were the Ghosts of people from the interior passing over on their way to the ocean.

One of our people was a 'Half Doctor'; he knew much medicine and was a good dancer. Once, when some one died, the 'Half Doctor' made up his mind that he would find out about the Ghost. So after dark he went to the place and hid close to the grave and watched. In the night he saw some- thing like a person get up out of the ground and shake his head to shake the earth off, and then fly away quickly, disappearing at once. Nothing more was seen.

WAH-TIB'-SAH THE SIGN OF DEATH

The Northern Mewuk of the Mokelumne River foothills say:

WHEN a person feels the inner side of the calf of his leg twitch, as if some one were poking it with his finger, it is a sure sign that within three days somebody is going to die, and he must take care that he is not the one. The twitching is done by the person's totem or guardian spirit, who comes and pokes his leg to warn him, of the danger. [1]

[My informant, the chief of a small rancheria, told me that he had been thus warned several times by Mā'-wā the Gray Squirrel, who was his totem, and that each time some one had died. He told me also that an old blind woman who lived in the rancheria, and whose totem was a Yellow-jacket wasp, had more than once saved his life by whispering to him just as he was going somewhere, that she had felt Wah-tib'-sah and he had better not go. Her totem friend, Mel'-ling-i'-yah the Yellow-jacket, had come and poked her leg to warn her that somebody must die. He had always heeded her warning and stayed at home and was still alive, while some one else, in a neighboring rancheria, had died.]

---

[1] For remarks on the prevalence and Significance of totemism among the Mewan tribes, see my article entitled "Totemism in California," American Anthropologist, vol. x, 558-561, 1908.

BELIEFS CONCERNING NATURAL PHENOMENA

THUNDER

The Northern Mewuk near South Fork Cosumnes River say:

TIM'-mel-le the Thunder is, or is like, Ti'-e-te the Valley Bluejay. He lives down below [west] in the San Joaquin Valley, where the clouds are. Sometimes he becomes angry and makes a great rumbling noise; this noise is Tim'-mel-le the Thunder. [1]

---

[1] For additional beliefs about Thunder, see First People stories, pages 79-81; 95.

THE RAINBOW

The Northern Mewuk say:

KU-yet'-tah the Rainbow comes to tell the people a baby is born. When anyone sees Ku-yet'-tah he knows that somewhere a new baby has come. Everybody knows that.

The Hookooeko of Nicasio and Tomales Bay say:

Kah-chah the Rainbow is the bow of O'-ye the Coyote-man.

THE EARTHQUAKE

The Olayome of Putah Creek say:

UNDER the earth is a great giant named He-wow'-wah-tin. When angry he shakes the earth, causing Yo'-wan-hew'-wah the Earth-quake.

NOISE

The Tuolumne Mewuk say:

IN the beginning all noise came from water--running water. [Their word for shouting is Wah-kah-lah'-loo, derived from Wah-kah'-loo, river.]

The Northern Mewuk also say:

All noise came in the beginning from running water; the echo originally came from rapids or boisterous water.

Other tribes say:

Singing came from running water--the first song was sung by the creek.

THE ECHO

The Hookooeko of Nicasio and Tomales Bay say:

PE-tān'-yah the Lizard with blue sides [1] lives everywhere in the rocks and hills and woods. When he hears a loud noise he talks back. This is Si-yu-kā-i the Echo; it is Pe-tān'-yah talking back.

The Olayome of Putah Creek say:

Loo-te'-nek'-kah the Echo is Pe-tā'-le the blue-sided Lizard talking back.

The Olamentko of Bodega Bay say:

The Echo is Sah-kah'-te talking back.

---

[1] The blue-sided lizard meant is Sceloporus occidentalis, a common species in the coast region of California.

HOW THE WORLD GREW

The Northern Mewuk say:

IN the beginning the world was rock. Every year the rains came and fell on the rock and washed off a little; this made earth. By and by plants grew on the earth and their leaves fell and made more earth. Then pine trees grew and their needles and cones fell every year and with the other leaves and bark made more earth and covered more of the rock.

If you look closely at the ground in the woods you will see how the top is leaves and bark and pine needles and cones, and how a little below the top these are matted together, and a little deeper are rotting and breaking up into earth. This is the way the world grew--and it is growing still.

BELIEFS CONCERNING WITCHES, PIGMIES, GIANTS, AND OTHER FABULOUS BEINGS

HOW WITCHES KILL PEOPLE

The Hookooeko of Nicasio and San Rafael say:

OUR country is on the north side of San Francisco Bay and reaches from San Rafael to Tomales Bay. Before the white man came and destroyed us there used to be witches among the people. The people used to burn the dead. Sometimes after a burning the witches would save the ashes and burnt bones (called me'-cham yem'-me-um) and pound them up fine in a stone mortar and use them to kill with. The witches had two ways of killing people. One way was to put the powdered bones and ashes on the windward side of the house or rancheria of the person they wished to harm. Then the wind would blow the fine dust over the enemy. Next day he would have a headache and feel sick, and every day grow worse until by and by he died.

Another way was to take the hollow wing bone of a Turkey-buzzard and go to windward of the person to be injured. The witch then blew through the bone toward the person. The person soon had bad dreams and felt lonesome, and next day went crazy, and after a while died. With the right kind of a buzzard bone (called to'-kah) a witch could blow harm to a person from a distance as great as two miles.

PIGMIES AND WATER PEOPLE

The Hookooeko of Nicasio and Tomales Bay say:

SE'-kah the Little Folk dwell in thick places in the dark redwood forest, where no people live. They are very small. Sometimes they make people crazy.

Le'-wah ke'-lak the Water People live in the ocean, in a roundhouse under the water; sometimes they come up and show themselves.

THE DEVIL OF SAN RAFAEL

The Hookooeko of San Rafael say:

YU'-ten me'-chah the Evil One lives in the hills just north of San Rafael; he travels about at night and sometimes comes and touches people when they are asleep, to frighten them.

HO-HĀ'-PE THE RIVER MERMAID

The Southern Mewuk of Merced River foothills say:

SOME of the rivers are inhabited by Ho-hā'-pe, the River Mermaids or Water Women. The Ho-ha'-pe have long hair and are beautiful to look at. They usually live in deep pools, and are known at several places in Wah-kal'-mut-tah (Merced River). In that part of the river which runs through Ah-wah'-ne (Yosemite Valley) they have been seen a number of times.

One lives now lower down in the river, at the upper end of Pleasant Valley in the large round pool called Ow'-wal. In the early days two partners used to fish for salmon at Ow'-wal, one on each side of the pool; several times they saw Ho-hā'-pe.

Another lives in the deep water at Wel'-le-to (on the Barrett ranch, a little below Pleasant Valley). At this place a few years ago some Indians from Bear Valley and Coulterville came to catch salmon. They put their net in a deep place in the river, and when it was full of fish tried to pull it out, but could not, for it was stuck on the bottom. Ho-hā'-pe the Water Woman had fastened it to a rock, but the men did not know this. One of them went down to find where the net had caught, and to lift it up. While he was doing this Ho-hā'-pe put a turn of the net-rope around his big toe and he was drowned. Then several of the men had to go down to get him. After they brought up his body all of them saw Ho-hā'-pe in the pool below, and saw her long hair float out in the current.

NOTE--The story of Ho-hā'-pe the River Mermaid, varying more or less in details, reaches north at least to American River, where the Nissenan (who call her Ho-sā'-pah) have the following version:

Two maidens were walking along American River below the foothills when they heard a baby cry. They followed the sound and soon saw the baby lying on a sand bar in the edge of the river. One of them reached down to pick it up when it suddenly changed to Ho-sā'-pah the River Mermaid, who, seizing the young woman, dragged her into the river. She cried out and her companion took hold of her arm and pulled and pulled as hard as she could to save her, but Ho-sā'-pah was the stronger and dragged her under the water and she was never seen again.

The other maiden ran home to the village and told her people what had happened. She was so terribly frightened that her mind became affected and in a short time she died.

THE ROCK GIANTS

CHE-HA-LUM'-CHE THE ROCK GIANT OF CALAVERAS COUNTY

Che-ha-lum'-che the Rock Giant catching People to eat

The Northern Mewuk say:

CHE-ha-lum'-che the Rock Giant carries on his back a big burden basket (che'-ka-la) which, like himself, is of rock. He lives in caves, of which there are two near Mountain Ranch or El Dorado in Calaveras County, one at Murphys, and one on Stanislaus River.

Che-ha-lum'-che comes out only at night and wanders about seeking Mewuk [people] to eat. He prefers women; of these he catches and carries off all he can find. Sometimes he makes a crying noise, hoo-oo'-oo like a baby, to lure them. If they come he seizes them and tosses them into his big pack basket and carries them to his cave, where he eats them. In the basket is a long spike which pierces their bodies when they are thrown in, so they can not escape.

In his caves are the remains of his victims--horns of deer and bones of people and different kinds of animals.

Indians never throw their dead into caves. If they did, Che-ha-lum'-che would get them. Any man who would put a dead person in a cave would be killed by the other Indians. [1]

---

[1] Many human skulls and skeletons have been found in eaves along the west slope of the middle Sierra. The presence of human remains in these caves has been interpreted to mean that the Indians now living in the region practise cave burial, or did practise it until recent times. This is an error. The Indians of this region, the Mewuk, burned their dead, and look with horror on the suggestion that they or their ancestors might ever have put their dead in caves. They ask: "Would you put your mother, or your wife, or your child, or any one you love, in a cave to be eaten by a horrible giant?" The idea is so abhorrent to them that the theory of cave burial must be abandoned as preposterous.

The mythology of the Mewuk does not admit of any migration but describes the creation of the people in the area they still inhabit. This, in connection with the fact that these Indians speak a language wholly different from any known in any other part of the world, proves that they have occupied the lands they now occupy for a very long period--a period--which in my judgment should be measured by thousands of years.

This argues a great antiquity for the cave remains, for they must be those of a people who inhabited the region before the Mewuk came--and this takes us back a very long way into the past.

OO'-LE THE ROCK GIANT OF THE CHOWCHILLA FOOTHILLS

The Southern Mewuk say:

FAR away in the west, in the place where the sun goes down, lived Oo'-le the Rock Giant. At night he used to come up into the foothills to catch people and eat them.

LOO'-POO-OI'-YES THE ROCK GIANT OF TAMALPAIS

The Hookooeko of Nicasio and San Rafael say:

A woman had a husband and two boy babies--twins. The woman's brother killed her husband and the little boys did not know that they ever had a father. When they were big enough they went off every day to play by a big rock in the woods. They went always to the same place; they liked this place and always went there. This was the very place where their father, when he was alive, used to go every day to sing, but the little boys did not know this--for they did not even know that they had ever had a father.

One day the boys heard somebody say: "You come here every day just as your father used to." The voice came from the rock; it was the voice of Loo'-poo-oi'-yes [1] the Rock Giant. Then the boys knew they had had a father. They went to the rock and saw long hairs sticking up. These hairs grew out of the nostrils of Loo'-poo-oi'-yes; the boys took hold of them and pulled them out.

This made Loo'-poo-oi'-yes angry and he took a long hooked stick and tried to catch the boys to kill them. He was all rock except a place on his throat where he wore an abalone shell. The boys, saw this and shot their arrows through it and killed him. When he died he fell to pieces; the pieces were rocks and scattered over the ground. Inside he was flesh like other people, but outside he was rock, except the place on his throat where the abalone shell was.

---

[1] The name Loo'-poo-oi'-yes means literally the old man of rock, from loo'poo rock, and oi'yes old man.

KĀ'-LUM-ME THE ROCK GIANT OF WENNOK VALLEY

The Olayome of Putah Creek say:

IN a cave under the cliff on the east face of Oo'-tel-tal-lah pow'-we, a small mountain southwest of the south end of Wennok Lake in Lake County, dwells Kā'-lum-me the Rock Giant. He used to roam about nights, catching Indians and carrying them off to his cave to eat. He has not done this for some time.

SCIENTIFIC NAMES OF THE ANIMALS

FOR purposes of exact identification the scientific names of the mammals, birds, reptiles and a few other animals mentioned in the text are here given. Most of these were originally First People; they turned into animals at or about the time real people were created.

The Indian names of the First People who turned into these animals are given at the beginning of each story.

MAMMALS

Antelope, Antilocapra americana

Badger, Taxidea taxus neglecta

Bear--See Black, Grizzly, and Cinnamon Bear

Black Bear, Ursus americanus (black phase)

Bobcat or Wildcat, Lynx fasciatus pallescens

Cinnamon Bear, Ursus americanus (brown or red phase)

Cougar, Felis hippolestes

Coyote, Canis ochropus

Deer, Columbia Blacktail, Odocoileus columbianus

Elk, Cervus nannodes (California Valley Elk)

Fox, See Gray Fox

Gopher, Thomomys--several species

Gray Tree Squirrel, Sciurus fossor

Grizzly Bear, Ursus horribilis californicus

Gray Fox, Urocyon californicus

Kangaroo Rat, Perodipus streatori (of the Sierra foothills

Mountain Lion--See Cougar

Raccoon, Procyon psora

Skunk (large kind, Mephitis occidentalis

Shrew, Sorex vagrans

Timber-wolf, Canis

Weasel, Putorius xanthogenys

White-footed Mouse, Peromyscus gambeli

Woodrat, Neotoma fuscipes streatori (of the Sierra foothills

BIRDS

Barn Owl, Aluco pratincola

Blackbird, Redwing, Agelaius (considered the male) and Brewer Blackbird, Euphagus (considered the female)

Bluejay, California, Aphelocoma californica

Bluejay, Mountain or Crested, Cyanocitta stelleri frontalis

Condor, Gymnogyps californianus

Crow, Corvus brachyrhynchos hesperis

Dove, Zenaidura macroura carolinensis

Eagle, Bald or White-headed, Haliæetus leucocephalus

Eagle, Golden, Aquila chrysaetos

Falcon, Peregrine or Duck-hawk, Falco peregrinus anatum

Falcon, Prairie, Falco mexicanus

Goose, Canada or Black-necked, Branta canadensis

Goose, Gray, Anser albifrons gambeli

Grebe (small) or Helldiver, Podilymbus podiceps

Heron, Great Blue, Ardea herodias

Humming-bird--several species

Mallard Duck, Anas platyrhynchos

Meadowlark, Sturnella neglecta

Nuthatch, Sitta carolinensis aculeata

Owl, Great Horned, Bubo virginianus pacificus

Quail, California, Lophortyx californicus

Raven, Corvus corax sinuatus

Red-shafted Flicker, Colaptes cafer collaris

Robin, Planesticus migratorius propinquus

Sandhill Crane, Grus mexicana

Sapsucker, Sphyrapicus ruber

Screech Owl, Otus asio bendirei

Spoonbill or Shoveler Duck, Spatula clypeata

Turkey Buzzard, Cathartes aura septentrionalis

Wren, Tule, Telmatodytes palustris paludicola

REPTILES

Frog, Rana draytoni

Lizard, Black, Sceloporus biseriatus (black phase)

Lizard, Blue-sided, Sceloporus occidentalis

Lizard, Fire, Crotophytus silus

Lizard, Little, Sceloporus graciosus

Rattlesnake, Crotalus lucifer

Toad, Bufo halophilus

Turtle, Clemmys marmorata

INSECTS AND OTHER INVERTEBRATES

Common Fly--several species

Poison Spider, Lathrodectus mactens

Yellowjacket Wasp, Vespa (several species)

Money Clam (thick northern species), Saxidomus giganteus

Money Clam (common species), Saxidomus nuttalli

Abalone, Haliotis (several species)

SCIENTIFIC NAMES OF THE TREES AND OTHER PLANTS

Buckeye, Aesculus californica

Buttonball bush, Cephalanthus occidentalis

Cane or Reed, Phragmites vulgaris

Cedar, Incense, Libocedrus decurrens

Elderberry, Sambucus glauca

Madrone, Arbutus menziesi

Manzanita, Arctostaphylos (several species)

Oak, Black, Quercus californica

Oak, Blue, Quercus douglasi

Oak, Valley or Water, Quercus lobata

Pine, Digger, Pinus sabiniana

Pine, Sugar, Pinus lambertiana

Pine, Yellow, Pinus ponderosa

Sage-herb, Artemisia ludoviciana

Sycamore, Platinus racemosa

BIBLIOGRAPHY OF CALIFORNIA MYTHOLOGY[1]

BARRETT, S. A. "A Composite Myth of the Pomo Indians," in the Journal of American Folk-lore (Boston, 1906), vol. xix, 37-51.

BOSCANA. "Chinigchinich" [Luiseño] in A. Robinson's Life in California (New York, 1846).

BURNS, L. M. "'Digger' Indian Legends" [Scott Valley Shasta], in Land of Sunshine (Los Angeles, 1901), vol. xiv, 130-134; 223-226; 310-314; 397-402.

CHAMBERS, G. A. [Fragment of a Mermaid story from the Chico Midoo), in the Journal of American Folk-lore (1906), vol. xix, 141.

CLARK, GALEN. Indians of Yosemite Valley [Southern Mewuk], (Yosemite Valley, Calif., 1904), chap. vii, "Myths and Legends."

CURTIN, JEREMIAH. Creation Myths of Primitive America [Wintoon and Yana tribes], (Boston, 1898).

------ Achomawi Myths, edited by Roland Dixon, in Journal of American Folk-lore (1909), vol. xxii, 283-287.

DENNY, MELCENA BURNS. "Orleans Indian Legends" [Karok or Kworatem], in Out West (Los Angeles, Calif.), vol. xxv (1906), 37-40; 161-166; 268-271; 373-375; 451-454; vol. xxvi (1907), 73-80; 168-170; 267-268.

DIXON, ROLAND B. "Some Coyote Stories from the Maidu Indians of California," in the Journal of American Folk-lore (1900), vol. xiii, 267-270.

DIXON, ROLAND B. "Maidu Myths," in the American Museum of Natural History Bulletin (New York, 1902), vol. xvii, part ii, 33-118.

---

[1] Ethnologists and others should take greater care in the identification of the personages mentioned in the myths. The value of many of the papers whose titles are here given is materially lessened by false identifications of the animal people.

------ "System and Sequence in Maidu Mythology," in the Journal of American Folk-lore (1903), vol. xvi, 32-36.

------ "Mythology of the Shasta-Achomawi," in the American Anthropologist (Washington, D.C., 1905), vol. vii, 607-612.

------ "Achomawi and Atsugewi Tales," in the Journal of American Folk-lore (1908), vol. xxi, 159-177.

DuBOIS, CONSTANCE GODDARD. "Mythology of the Diegueños," in the Journal of American Folk-lore (1901), vol. xiv, 181-185.

------- "The Story of Chaup: A Myth of the Diegueños," in the Journal of American Folk-lore (1904), vol. xvii, 217-242.

"Mythology of the [Luiseño] Mission Indians," in the Journal of American Folk-lore, vol. xvii (1904), 185-188; vol. xix (1906), 52-6o; 145-164.

------ "The Raven of Capistrano" [Luiseño], in Out West (1907), vol. xxvi, 430-437; 537-544; vol. xxvii, 57-64; 152157; 227-233; 343-351; 415-421; 523-531.

------ "Religion of the Luiseño Indians of Southern California. Myths," in the California University publications on American Archæology and Ethnology (Berkeley, Calif., 1908), vol. viii, 128-157.

------ "The Spirit Wife--A Mission Myth (elaborated)," in the Southern Workman (Hampton, Va., 1908), vol. xxxvii, 477-480; 512.

------ "Ceremonies and Traditions of the Diegueño Indians" [with fragment of a Yuma creation myth], in the Journal of American Folk-lore (1908), vol. xxi, 228-236.

GODDARD, PLINY EARLE. "Hupa Texts," in the California University publications on American Archæology and Ethnology (1904), vol. i.

GODDARD, PLINY EARLE. "Lassik Tales," in the Journal of American Folk-lore (1906), vol. xix, 133-140.

------ "Kato Texts. Translations," in the California University publications on American Archæology and Ethnology (1909), vol. v, 183-238.

HARRINGTON, JOHN PEABODY. "A Yuma Account of Origins," in the Journal of American Folk-lore (1908), vol. xxi, 324-338.

HUDSON, J. W. "An Indian [Yokut] Myth of the San Joaquin Basin," in the Journal of American Folk-lore (1902), vol. xv, 104-106.

JOHNSTON, ADAM. [Fragment of a "Po-to-yan-te" Yokut Creation Myth] in H. R. Schoolcraft's Indian Tribes (Washington, D.C., 1854), vol. iv, 224-225.

KROEBER, A. L. "Wishosk Myths," in the Journal of American Folk-lore (1905), vol. xviii, 85-107-

------ "Indian Myths of South Central California," [1] in the California University Publications on American Archæology and Ethnology (1907), vol. iv, 169-250.

------ "Origin Tradition of the Chemehuevi Indians," in the Journal of American Folk-lore (1908), vol. xxi, 240-242.

------ "Two Myths of the [Luiseño] Mission Indians of California," in the Journal of American Folk-lore (1906), vol. xix, 309-321.

------ Notes on California Folk-lore. [A Luiseño Tale; Wiyot Folk-lore], in the Journal of American Folk-lore (1908), vol. xxi, 35-39.

KROEBER, HENRIETTE ROTHSCHILD. "Wappo Myths" [The Two Brothers; The Coyote and the Frog], in the Journal of American Folk-lore (1908), vol. xxi, 321-323.

------ "California Indian Legends" [The Pleaides, a "Southern California" Myth; The Theft of Fire, a Yokut Myth], in Out West (1908), vol. xxviii, 66-69.

---

[1] Mainly Yokut, but comprising also six important fragments of"Rumsien Costanoan" [Kah'-koon A-chēs-ta], four second-hand fragments of "Pohonichi Miwok" [Southern Mewuk], and one "Gitanemuk Shoshonian" [Ke'-tah-na-mwa-kam or Tejon Serrano].

POWERS, STEPHEN. Tribes of California (Contributions to North American Ethnology, Washington, D.C., 1877), vol. iii.

Contains myths of several tribes, very loosely rendered.

RIED, HUGO. [Fragments of Gabrielino or Tong-vā Myths, collected in 1852], in the Essex Institute Bulletin (Salem, Mass., 1885), vol. xvii, 15-17; 18-26.

SPARKMAN, P. S. "A Luiseño Tale," in the Journal of American Folk-lore (1908), vol. xxi, 35-36.

SPENCER, D. L. "Notes on the Maidu Indians of Butte County, California" [The Buumo Myth--Battle of the Coyote and Bat], in the Journal of American Folk-lore (1908), vol. xxi, 244-245.

STEWART, GEO. W. "Two Yokuts Traditions" [Fragments of Tache tales on the Origin of Fire, and the Turtle], in the Journal of American Folk-lore (1908), vol. xxi, 237-239.

"A Yokuts [Wiktchumne] Creation Myth," in the Journal of American Folk-lore (1906), vol. xix, 322.

WATERMAN, THOMAS. Analysis of the Mission Indian Creation Story, in the American Anthropologist (1909), vol. xi, 41-55.

NOTE. The author's manuscript of the bibliography has been altered somewhat in form to agree with the form preferred by the publisher.

www.ingramcontent.com/pod-product-compliance
Lightning Source LLC
Chambersburg PA
CBHW061103100726
47911CB00012B/376